MOTTI

D1413967

OTHER WORKS IN
DALKEY ARCHIVE PRESS'S
HEBREW LITERATURE SERIES

Dolly City
Orly Castel-Bloom

Heatwave and Crazy Birds
Gabriela Avigur-Rotem

Homesick
Eshkol Nevo

Life on Sandpaper
Yoram Kaniuk

MOTTI

a novel by

ASAF

SCHURR

TRANSLATED AND WITH AN
AFTERWORD BY TODD HASAK-LOWY

Series Editor: Rachel S. Harris

DALKEY ARCHIVE PRESS
CHAMPAIGN AND LONDON

Originally published in Hebrew as *Motti* by Babel, Tel Aviv, 2008
Copyright © 2008 by Asaf Schurr
English translation © by the Institute for the Translation of Hebrew Literature
Published by arrangement with the Institute for the Translation of Hebrew Literature
First edition, 2011
All rights reserved

Library of Congress Cataloging-in-Publication Data

Shur, Asaf.
  [Moti. English]
  Motti : a novel / by Asaf Schurr ; translated and with an afterword by Todd Hasak-Lowy. -- 1st ed.
      p. cm.
  ISBN 978-1-56478-642-5 (pbk. : alk. paper)
  I. Hasak-Lowy, Todd, 1969- II. Title.
  PJ5055.41.U733M6813 2011
  892.4'37--dc22
                              2011002839

Partially funded by the University of Illinois at Urbana-Champaign and by a grant from the
Illinois Arts Council, a state agency

The Hebrew Literature Series is published in collaboration with the Institute for the Translation
of Hebrew Literature and sponsored by the Office of Cultural Affairs, Consulate General of
Israel in New York

www.dalkeyarchive.com

Cover: design and composition by Danielle Dutton, photo from the Russian Space Agency
Printed on permanent/durable acid-free paper and bound in the United States of America

To good Cookie
As you embark on a new path

MOTTI

Structurally, this book is strict. Strict and very simple. A symmetrical pyramid with a summit of clouds and a base of Euclidian geometry. Nevertheless, it's a book, not a concert or some sort of performing art, I don't get the chance to sit in the theater and offer suggestions during rehearsals. And there's no division between the audience and the stage. You're the performers and the audience all at once, and everything is already out of my control. Therefore I can only request that you read attentively, or at least not with complete indifference. Even with joy, perhaps, those paragraphs worthy of it. From my perspective it's all the same now. At any rate, I do not know and will never know most of you, and if you die (even in the middle of a chapter) I'll never know a thing about it.

Yes, that's how it is. In our own eyes we're very important, but for almost everyone else our death won't even warrant a few lines in the local paper. Think of all the people you pass on the street every week. Some of them have already died, and you didn't even notice. And we will too, some day, and our absence won't be felt by those who remain, walking the streets in the evening, out with the dog, or on the way to the trash with a big bag of garbage.

And because of this the simplicity. Because of this. There are almost no games here, no deception, there is no deviousness at all in this book. No manipulation. Everything is simple as can be. Everything is on the table. The cards are on the table, the tablecloth is on the table, everything is on the table, open the refrigerator, there's nothing in it, everything is on the table, everything, look underneath, nothing there either, everything is on the table and in midair the table stands.

FIRST

OUTSIDE

Sure, I hate to paint. First of all it's work, second it's smelly, third it's a mess, fourth it takes up space. Don't like to paint. I paint only when I have to.

—Rafi Lavi in an interview with Dana Gillerman, *Haaretz*

All propositions are results of truth-operations on the elementary propositions.

The truth-operation is the way in which a truth-function arises from elementary propositions.

According to the nature of truth-operations, in the same way as out of elementary propositions arise their truth-functions, from truth-functions arises a new one. Every truth-operation creates from truth-functions of elementary propositions another truth-function of elementary propositions, i.e. a proposition. The result of every truth-operation on the results of truth-operations on elementary propositions is also the result of one truth-operation on elementary propositions.

Every proposition is the result of truth-operations on elementary propositions.

—Ludwig Wittgenstein, *Tractatus Logico-Philosophicus*

1

Motti loved Menachem like a brother. That is, despite himself.

Perhaps they met in the army. This is not uncommon among Israelis. Perhaps they met before that, in school. Possibly even in college. Yet from the very beginning, the balance of power was clear. Menachem always had the upper hand, even when this hand was patting his friend's shoulder.

This is how it is: Like a smack across a dog's snout, the first meeting of two people can determine the structure, the shared soul, of their relationship. It carves a pattern in them, cuts a path like water through a stone (it scars, in other words). And once a balance of power is set, no lever, no matter how strong, will ever shift it. Even among wolf packs the hierarchy is more fluid than among humans, who, steeped in our habits and laws, never budge from a pattern, once established. And if Motti and Menachem really did meet in the army, it's obvious which one of them was the commanding officer. Obvious, because despite the many years that have passed since then, this rule was scorched into Motti and hasn't faded. Sure, part of him understands that the Menachem he knew back then—always screaming and always punishing and all powerful; it was safer to stick close to him at all times, since otherwise he could pop up suddenly and give an order, could punish you for anything—that this Menachem was wearing a mask, and that the real Menachem is the one he knows now, his good friend Menachem. Yet even though he knows this, Motti has still never truly convinced himself, over the course of all the years since (they've spent a hundred hours together as friends for each difficult hour they had back then), that then it was only a mask, while this is now Menachem's true face. At any moment, he fears, Menachem's face is liable to fall away from him like so many dirty clothes, revealing the old, remembered features below. At any moment he could start abusing Motti like he used to, and Motti would obey.

Motti's willingness to obey, along with his courtesy, provided him a wonderful buffer, the way electric fences leave an uncontaminated area all around. Breathing room. No one can enter here, he told himself, worried he needed this space, afraid that others would hurt him. Never admitting to himself the real reason for keeping this distance: that he ascribed so much importance to himself that he felt the slightest act on his part might cause someone else grievous injury.

What are you doing tonight? Menachem asked over the telephone. I was thinking about leaving Edna at home with the little ones and going out for a drink. Are you with me? Pick you up at your place at eight thirty?

Sure, Motti said to him. Eight thirty.

Ya'alla, Menachem said. Eight thirty. I'm fucking crazy about you.

I love you, too, my brother, Motti said.

Hey, man, are you turning fag on me or what?

Nah, Motti said, I was just talking. I didn't mean it. I just wanted to see how it rolled off the tongue.

And that's the problem: even though all true expressions are a matter of rolling, not all true problems are a matter of expression—and yet, many problems stem precisely from this, that is, from the desire to see how they roll. Because from the moment it becomes possible to say a thing, even something untrue, it becomes necessary to say it, to let it roll, and so it takes on motion and expands, and let's see you try to stop it then (impossible). And the moment it's spoken and comes into being, it's a beautiful and common mistake to think that maybe it's true. But we can say all sorts of things, wonderful things. It doesn't mean a thing. But the temptation—oh, the temptation—to say them (and the need to believe them)!

2

He sits next to the table and reads the paper, his cell phone disman-
tled and slowly drying on the business section (before, when he
was done speaking with Menachem, it fell right into the sink). His
beloved dog Laika rests her head on his thigh, and he scratches behind her right ear absentmindedly. Then her ears stand up and she
hurries to the door; a moment later Motti too hears Ariella's keys
jingling as she comes up the stairs. Excited, like Laika, he hurries
to greet her. One must be prepared: he gathers up the garbage bag
from the can, and before she arrives at the door he's already there.
Turns the bolt and opens. She comes up the stairs toward him, her
colorful handbag on her shoulder. He hurries to her, and she raises
her eyes to him and smiles.

Hi, Ariella.

Again she smiles at him, a small set of keys in her hand.

Laika missed you, he says and hurries down the stairs. Laika's
tail wags from behind the closed door, and sensitive as Motti is to
this sound, his sleeve is so close to Ariella's hair as they pass by one
another. Patience is a virtue. A wonderful virtue. Motti will wait as
long as he has to. His real life waits, concealed inside the future like
a jewel in a thick cloth.

Meanwhile she goes up the stairs, the key already in her hand. She opens the door and goes inside, turns and smiles at him before being closed inside the apartment. After taking out the trash Motti will stand again for a moment next to the living room wall, this being the wall that separates his place from hers. The cold wall on his cheek, he breathes deeply. Patient. Every day, over and over again, his heart breaks. (Every day. It's a biological miracle.) Over and over again his heart breaks and light pours inside, glowing or whatever light does from inside this abyss, this rift that has opened inside him.

In the evening Menachem came and they went out drinking. They didn't talk about anything of much importance, and Menachem often slapped Motti on the back and talked about fucking and laughed loudly. Motti paid for both their beers, and afterward returned home and went out for a walk with Laika. She sniffed around the garbage cans longer than usual, and he peeked at his watch every second to make sure that he'd manage to sleep six and a half hours exactly, that he'd manage to drink coffee and take a quick shower before the time that Ariella would leave her apartment, that he would again manage to see her on the stairs. A day will come when he'll speak to her for real, but in the meantime there's no rush.

They went to sleep, the two of them, Laika and Motti. And he hurried to fall asleep, so that he wouldn't find himself unoccupied, lost inside a forest of minutes in which there's nothing to do. Before dawn, Laika whimpered as though she'd had a bad dream. Still asleep, his hand descended. He petted her, she calmed down, fell asleep again. My little wolf pack, that's what he calls her. My little wolf pack.

3

In the morning, since his first class was cancelled, he was late leaving. Drank coffee next to the window looking out on the street. And that's why he was there, honestly, just an accident, when Ariella was leaving the apartment. Followed her with his eyes as she went away down the sidewalk alone, until she disappeared from sight. Years from now perhaps they'll leave the building like this, together. They'll walk hand in hand until the end of the street, and then they'll kiss and turn away to go about their business. During work he'll think of her. Full of happiness and satisfaction he'll attend to his classes, in a good mood, in high spirits. During the break he'll sit in the teachers' lounge, but he won't talk about her. Relationships are a personal matter. Though it's not impossible that they, him and her together, will befriend another couple (this in addition to Menachem and Edna, with whom they'll perhaps go on vacation once or twice a year). Sometimes they'll meet at home, for dinner and a pleasant conversation and cake and coffee, sometimes they'll go to a movie. The kind of movies there are sure to be by then! Out of the world special effects. Though sometimes they'll happen upon some foreign film at a small movie house (or at the Cinémathèque). After the movie they'll go drink a glass of wine somewhere nearby, and if he worried less about her getting sick or hurt, they'd also smoke cigarettes, French ones even.

And on other days, at home, many years from now, they won't meet with anyone and won't go anywhere special. They'll get home at the end of the workday and have a bite to eat. They'll go out together to the street each evening, for a relaxing walk with Laika. No, not with Laika. Many years from now we said, and by then Laika will already be dead (tears well up at the thought, but he doesn't cry), okay, not with Laika, maybe a different dog, a different female, one of her offspring, why not, even though she was already spayed long ago, it would take a miracle, but this too is possible, indeed miracles fall on the world like rain, you need only to catch one and not let go.

4

Whoever isn't familiar with the details, or didn't take an active part in the Soviet space program, is liable to think that Laika's body burned up as it reentered the atmosphere. Just a few hours she spent in space, and within a short time she died. Afterward, it was hinted that her food was poisoned, that her air ran out as planned, that this was a mercy killing, so she wouldn't suffer from the great heat of the friction between the spaceship's side panels and the atmosphere, the atmosphere that, in principle, allows us to live, even though in this instance the opposite would be true. Later on it was said that she did in fact die from the heat after all, despite all precautions, something went wrong with the spaceship, something got screwed up, we apologize for this regrettable incident.

But no, it wasn't so simple. How could Laika's soul leave her body in such a quotidian way? After all, she wasn't only the first living being to go into orbit—she was also the first to die there. The first to sow the seeds of death in what was already a gaping expanse of death: an offering to the big nothing. Like ancient tribesmen we sent her into the darkness ahead of us, to appease whatever is out there, so it wouldn't take whomever would follow, sealed in a closed metal case within a darkness wide as wide can be. (Indeed, there wasn't even a window. Entirely enclosed, confined to a narrow, forsaken space, absolutely miniscule, inside that other, wide-open space.)

It doesn't matter what time it happened, the clock slices time up arbitrarily, and even that it only does beneath the skies, not above them. The dog, a stray, was restless, was frightened when strapped into its harness, when the engines were fired. When the acceleration flattened her, she was terrified. Did she actually know what was happening there? Did she know, as everyone around her knew—all the people petting and training and feeding her, and then the ones measuring and preparing and keeping her healthy—that she would die in a moment? Doubtful she knew. ("A strange lightness envelops her," Ben Vered wrote, "her ears float in the little cell, and so do her legs and tail." So he wrote, but I myself don't believe it. I saw the apparatus she was harnessed into—they restrained her so tightly there wasn't room for her legs to float, and not her tail either. Her ears, perhaps.) Did she understand the source of the great pressure, and then the source of the terrible, increasing heat? Doubtful she understood. Did she wish that her fur might fall out everywhere, forming strands that would encircle the spaceship, like the stubble clinging to a bald man's head after a trim? Doubtful that she did. Instead, before she died, before she suffocated, perhaps (desperate for air), before she was cooked in her own skin, the inner heavens opened and a great light spilled out. A pleasure that was greater even than a treat. Greater than running in a field, even though she never enjoyed such a run; they took her straight from the cold streets of Moscow to the lab.

As if kind hands reached out and released her from her body (her bones remained, as clean as clean can be, to drift through space). Never before had she been so embraced. Her spiritual fur sparkled from such pleasure, and her spiritual tail wagged as if she was at play. She saw the light that persisted even within the absolute darkness of space, and small growls of excitement and expectation, satisfaction even, broke out from inside her spiritual throat. (Or so Motti thinks, now appeased. He's always like this. Stories that never happened and small mysteries, too—even those strange personal questionnaires in the newspaper, they always bother him. He never approaches them casually. Always so serious.) Laika was released from her body, from everything, she's quite free now, absolutely free, free to do as she pleases, no, freer even than that, she is even free from the fetters of her own desire.

Did she bark? I have to know if she barked. And how the echo sounded in that narrow space. If it sounded like distant dogs answering her.

We also close up space so that voices can echo—but whose voice? The events of the world (the world itself) are woven into a living network of overlapping dimensions. Motti's fingers of thought are sent toward things past like the fingers of a weaver wanting to try something different, to free each strand from an unsightly tapestry one knot at a time, to strive for something marvelous and new.

5

He will lie on his back in their bed, the bed that is theirs, and she'll take the thick pen resting on the nightstand right next to the bed, and she'll say, turn over. So he'll lie on his stomach in their bed, in the bed that is theirs, and she will write on his back, with the thick pen, property of Ariella. This here Motti is private and nontransferable. This Motti left our factory in good condition. This side up. Private. Not to be consumed after expiration date. Does not contain preservatives. Motti, for me and mine. Mine mine mine.

It will be like in that movie, what's it called. He'll tell her, that tickles, what are you writing? And she'll read to him. Which hand does she write with, right or left? Let's say right. She'll read to him and he'll add, we thank you for choosing Motti. Motti, for you and yours. Caution, fragile.

Good God! He could learn to make things with his hands! He'll make her necklaces, bracelets, chains, he'll make everything she needs. He'll do woodworking. He'll make her a pencil case if she needs one. He'll sew her a stethoscope case. A case for things you use to mark trails, for drawing maps, for veterinary medicine, for particle acceleration, for social work, for the philosophy of science, for the repair of electrical devices. He'll sew her a dress, a shirt, bell-bottom pants, a lunch bag for breaks at school (if she becomes a teacher, that is).

21

6

That's the way it is. Best for him, for Motti, are doorways. Sitting in a waiting room, bent over his number in line, sitting in a corridor with no one demanding anything, with no one glancing over his shoulder, no one telling him off or praising him. A certain amount of tension is a given with him, without his even thinking about it, like a fish in water or a man in the atmosphere, so it dissipates: the rules are known, and he doesn't have to do anything at all.

It accumulated in him, what else is there to say. It accumulated like bits of asbestos in the lungs of a fiber factory worker, sooner or later it'll reach a critical level. How much misery and frustration can one actually take? (And the answer, of course, is a lot, quite a lot. Entire long lives of this, and no creature will compensate Motti for it afterward, when the pulsing biological system—that is, his living, active body—shuts down. This will be his wasted life. His life and that's it. All this in small, ongoing portions, you get used to it. Only occasional little symptoms, sighs of dissatisfaction, and barely even a hint that anything else is possible, that there's a life of comfort and freedom out there, that there might be a place to relax in.) He didn't believe in great acts. Didn't believe in his ability to break through the tedious maze that is his life, to shatter the structure once and for all, his habits, his personality (every sort of behavior can be reinforced and encouraged, rewarded bit by bit until it becomes second nature; who would have guessed that it's possible to reinforce unbehavior in this way too?).

At first he would watch movies on video. Night after night, in front of the screen. Here too, time is beyond his control: on the faint display the digits turn over backward. Meanwhile he sits idly, his thoughts can either wander or not wander, drawn into the plot and then popping out again, free, and that's how it is again and again, there isn't a single constraint or necessity, just the silence of time. That's how it was at first, but after some time his attention began to wander to the supporting actors. The thought wouldn't leave him alone. Certainly they studied acting for years, waited for their chance, embarrassed themselves in children's plays, prayed over every tenth-rate part in a commercial on some local channel. So, again, he lost track of the plot, and now the lead actors as well. He couldn't take it anymore. Sometimes the supporting cast was more talented than the leads. Sometimes their noses were too big, or they looked too much like someone famous, and who needs two Harrison Fords, Brad Pitts, or Moshe Ivgys? Maybe one of them was an old woman by the time she got a part in a movie. Maybe she'd dreamed about acting since she was seven. Here, after years of frustration behind a counter at a shitty hotel (alternatively, a counter at some tax or transportation office, or any other office, unfulfilling but sadly not a temp job), she's finally got a part, at last facing the camera. Motti sat in the dark and cried bitterly, and then he sat in the dark and watched the film's credits until the end. So many people worked so hard, got home late, their children already tucked into bed and asleep, their spouses possibly cheating on them out of loneliness—and what, a man can't even spare the time necessary to redeem them, even without their knowing, to read their names and give thanks? Art is a letter written on the surface of time— someone wrote it, how can we not read it? But also over the following nights he remains sitting facing the credits and then facing the empty screen, waiting. He doesn't watch movies the way I did in my own childhood, with the thought that maybe they hid secret messages there, at the end of the movie, on the end of the reel, and that maybe a wild adventure would spin out from them. He doesn't watch that way. And if anyone could see him from outside, they might think that he's a sick man, a very unfortunate man, sitting in the dark and rocking absentmindedly back and forth in his chair. But looks from the outside are not to be trusted.

7

Whereas Menachem, absentmindedly, had made his life into a tangled net of debts and counterdebts. In fact, he made these debts into a kind of insurance for himself: as long as one of them is pending, as long as his attention is taken up with a grocery tab as yet unpaid, with an insignificant loan (a few shekels to be exact, which he took from a friend at work for the sake of the soda machine in the kitchenette), as long as his attention is taken up with some kind regards he was asked to pass along and that have not yet reached their destination—he cannot leave this world, and should this system fail him, should his death come without warning nevertheless, certainly these debts will bind his soul to this world, and he won't be able to depart, not without making prior arrangements. That's it, I think—if I can say I truly understand his motives. Actions are clear, those are what keep the book's plot moving, but motives, look, maybe I'm wrong and he acts this way for no particular reason, but there have to be motives, the kind we can understand, even identify with, and through this feel some sort of affinity with Menachem, maybe even affection, but his debts are debts in any event, and in the meantime Edna and Menachem are in bed, sleepy. Saturday morning and the kids are in the doorway, sneaking toward the bed to wake them gently. Note the frantic bustling under the blankets now, because last night there was a different sort of frantic bustling, and now Edna wants—without ruining the game by waking up ahead of time—to quickly, quickly pull on a pair of panties before the children crawl under the covers. She succeeds in the nick of time. The morning again opens with a family hug. And this, ladies and gentlemen, this is happiness. This is the quiet and relatively stable happiness of the members of this family. Menachem is willing to do exceptional things to maintain it, though frankly it might be advisable that he begin with simpler stuff, like for example not driving even a little bit drunk again. Idiot. His little friend Motti—this is how Menachem sees him, as his little friend, for no real reason, even though Motti is two months older than him and almost a head taller—also tells him this each and every time, don't drive drunk, you idiot. And there the voice of the narrator is bursting from Motti's throat. Not because driving under the influence is against the law (not at all for this reason—quite the contrary; I piss on the law, I fear it, I fear its blind power, and yet I piss on it), but rather because it's a matter, you know, of fractions of a second, running over a person or a dog or a cat or not running them over, braking in time. If someone, because he was drinking or just being careless, kills someone I love in this way, I'll put my hand so far up his ass he'll be sorry he was ever born. Unpleasant words.

Now, I know, I even hope, that there are those who are saying, and not unjustifiably: enough, I'm sick of this already. This writer guy already stuck himself into his last book more than enough, so why not do us a favor and leave us alone. Let the plot roll along and that's it. But me, what can I do? This is how I am, gentlemen. As my sister-in-law said to me on the same subject, if art has any obligation, if the people trying to make it have any obligation at all, it's only to be utterly human. That is, fully. And this includes being the piece of shit that this one is, overall—a pest, a nuisance, an irritation, etc.

And if I may, know that I don't do this out of arrogance (nor, I should admit, out of an overabundance of humility). I write like I write to upset my own sensitivities (write clean to upset my sensitivity to dirtiness, write dirty to upset my sensitivity to cleanliness—to annoy them just so, word by word. Because here, and not in my strange monologues, not in the various plotlines, in the possibility whose realization would be an unforgivable sin—no, no—here is the seed. The heart is the sentence. Always the sentence. It doesn't even matter what I say in it, it's just the labor that's important, always this labor, word after word after word, in the end a great light shines out from this, no, a small light, or not even that, but a light nevertheless, let's be satisfied with what we have. And if not a light, not even a flicker, something nevertheless happens. Some feeling is passed along, some idea. There is communication. Something is opened, we are mixed together like clear water poured from glass to glass).

8

They'll also buy a video camera. Maybe they'll have a boy. Or perhaps a girl. They'll record her in public places. At first, when she grows up and sees it, she'll be embarrassed. Years later, though, she'll be delighted. All the more so if she becomes a performance artist. So much material there for her to discover, her first words, her first steps. The last ones, they won't be there—Motti and Ariella—to record.

And Ariella, Ariella, with him she'll live like a queen. No. Not like a queen. Like a princess, who knows that the best is still to come. Again and always it is still ahead of her, everything just gets better and better. The finest crown he will set on her head, tender as a spring day, soft as moonlight, though not as sad. Oh my, how much he'll love her. Like children they'll go to an amusement park for fun, and he'll buy her cotton candy, and when her lips are sweet from sugar, he'll kiss her again and they'll laugh. Afterward they'll stand in line for the rollercoaster, maybe she'll wear heels in honor of this special day and she'll be taller than him. All the little kids will look at them, how much fun they have, laughing like crazy people on the way down, holding on to the safety bar so very tight and choking on this tiny pleasure. All the fathers of all the little kids will look at them in envy, they'll know that love like this can't be gotten just anywhere, the love that pop stars sing about without knowing what they're singing about, they'll know that she is his only, and he is hers. And at night they'll be together in bed, doing things you couldn't imagine. And if they find a boy that got lost there (not in bed, in the amusement park), maybe his mother went inside the public restroom for just a moment, and he, mistakenly, thought he saw her from a distance, so he went after her and now he's lost and frightened, Ariella will bend over and calm him down with some pleasant words, and together they'll all go and find the lost mother. She'll almost hyperventilate with relief, the mother, and the boy will say, Mommy, mommy, this pretty lady took care of me. And he, Motti, will stand back a bit as happy words are exchanged. Every week he'll bring home flowers for her, for her he'll fill beautiful vases and bring other little cheery gifts. At night (it's the best at night, more than anything he loves to return there in his thoughts) they lay their heads close on a pillow and talk, and he'll caress her under her nightgown or her pajamas or whatever she chooses to wear, unless she actually sleeps naked, then he'll caress, simply, the body that there's still no guessing how it will look or smell, what it will taste like on his tongue. During days off (sometimes in his imagination every day is a day off) they'll head out to nature and sometimes they'll stay home and sometimes they'll return to the amusement park, and one time the boy they saved from being lost will see them and run to them from far off, he'll hug Ariella with joy, and Motti will be happy too.

And at night (again the night, yes) they'll lay head beside head on a pillow, and the conversation will grow like a tree of many branches. Head beside head they'll lay them, and stare happily. You could make a ruler using the line that will stretch out between their eyes, between his pupils and her pupils, and the other way around at the same time. Though the question is if this is really possible in the first place—is it possible, that is, that we can ever truly speak, that we can see one another eye to eye—or if everything is like Motti and Menachem, someone always up and someone down, dominant and submissive. Maybe we're like wolf packs (in a positive sense, actually): there's an order to things, flexible to a certain extent; in other words, first one can be up and then the other can too, but there must always be both an up and a down. Only this keeps us moving. Only this lets us touch.

9

At night Laika woke up. Small movements passed through Motti's hand resting on her head during sleep, as if a small motor there had started up, and he woke as well. Each one lay in his or her place and listened. He heard nothing, and said to her, drowsy, Laika, enough. Quiet, Laika, quiet down. But she didn't quiet down. Her ears stood up. She growled. She listened for a moment and then jumped from her spot and rushed to the door. He wanted to go back to sleep, but she started to bark, and it's the middle of the night now, what about the neighbors. Stepped after her in the dark. Next to the door she wouldn't give him even a glance. Barked and barked at the door, maybe out of anger, maybe out of excitement, he doesn't know. Froze in her place for a moment and then once more, barking and barking like crazy and attacking the door, then she stops again and brings her snout close to the floor, as if she's trying to dig there, to squeeze through the sealed slit at the bottom of the door. What's there, Laika? (He asks her, but knows that she can't answer, since she's a dog, and not a person.) What's there, Laika? Quiet, Laika (he's scolding her). Quiet! It's the middle of the night.

She doesn't quiet down, and through the peephole there's only darkness. His cheek is up against the door and his eye to the eyepiece, and Laika sits down and fixes him with a glare. Who's there Laika? (He's asking again, and when she doesn't answer, he cautiously opens the door.) No one's there. Laika goes out and busily sniffs up and down the stairs. What is it, Laika? he asks her in a whisper in the stairwell and turns on the light. Who was here, girl?

Laika raises her eyes to him and crouches to urinate a bit next to the welcome mat. Afterward she goes inside with a drooping tail and heads to her place in the bedroom. Not giving him so much as a glance. He looks at the stairs for another moment, and then goes inside, locks and bolts the door. You have to be careful; outside, the world gapes wide open.

10

Perhaps he'd wronged Laika when he turned on the light, he thinks as he lies in bed and doesn't fall asleep. He pets her and looks at her. She averts her eyes, perhaps seeking in this way not to register her complaint, perhaps seeking in this way to minimize his presence to her senses, to negate in this way the wound lurking inside her. Perhaps (he wants to laugh dismissively, but the thought already has a hold on him), perhaps until he himself looked, until that moment the King of the Dogs was there, on the other side. He can't be seen through a peephole, and he, Motti, instead of letting Laika be, scolded her and opened the door and ruined everything. That's the problem with relationships between species so different, biologically speaking: you simply can't know with any certainty. The great god of the dogs was there—Motti makes up a story for himself before falling asleep. The King of Dogs materialized there all by himself and then, just like that, melted away. Didn't use the stairs. And actually, Laika urinated as a sign of mourning.

Or else, she smelled a ghost, let's say (forgive him, Motti . . . his thoughts are wandering through the strange regions of pre-sleep). Once there was a woman in England who said this about her dog, and people from all over England came to see. Either he read this once in a newspaper, or he's dreaming it up now, hard to know. And beside this, the British, you know. Even if he only thought of it just now, there's no reason that this foggy story should be any less reliable than a newspaper. Stranger coincidences have happened, even if we're not always paying attention to them. In any case, all sorts of unfounded stuff makes it into in the newspaper, maybe someone makes those things up in bed at night too.

The King of Dogs? But seriously! More reasonable, though not by much, is that their visitor was the incarnation of the first Laika. The one in space. She became the intergalactic prophet of a highly advanced race, nothing like the sort of alien we'd think up. Such strange things, strange and unthinkable things, happen in this world, why not this? Every weird story, however juvenile, can come true if we just wait long enough. If we just think up enough stories, logic dictates that one of them will turn out to be true in the end. Such is the power of statistics, Motti thought, sleep already lost to him, and now he got out of bed again and went to the living room, then came back and turned on the light, turned it off and walked to the refrigerator, didn't find anything of interest inside, went to the living room and again sat in the chair next to the wall, and then his cheek grew cold pressed against the white paint and the base coat and then the plaster, the cinderblocks, the plaster on the other side, the paint on the other side, the other life twitching there. If Motti's brain were made out of gears and tiny screws and other mechanical elements like an old watch that someone slaved over for ages, anonymously, if his brain were like this, a single perfect click would have burst out then from the fragile mechanism and echoed through the apartment. Since his brain was not like this, however, a very, very long exhalation, almost a moan, came out of his mouth instead, and his body slackened ever so slightly.

11

But, after all, if there are ghosts and gods and sudden rescues, and if there are powerful and wonderful beings out in the universe, then why can't there be a prophet, and if there's a prophet, then why not a messenger, and if there are messengers, why shouldn't Laika, his Laika, why shouldn't she be one of them, what impressive and important adventures she'd have to look forward to. She'll save everyone. Motti too. She'll rescue homeless animals, punctured laboratory animals with electric wires hanging out of the holes drilled into them, animals about to be made into food, animals abused by children. In the end, thanks to her, there will be a great fellowship of all living things. That is to say, the great fellowship that already exists, but that we refuse to see and recognize, will be revealed. Motti will have a role as well, he imagines, laughing at himself. Even in your wildest dreams (he laughs), even in your most unrealistic visions, you're so small and petty. Still, you must have a role, huh? As if you do so very much in your real life. (For all his defects, Motti is not lacking in self-criticism.)

12

How great is the need to believe, even to know with certainty, that there is someone above us who oversees, who determines, who keeps a watchful eye on every deed. To know that there is a father, an evil father even, just so long as he's there. Just so we'll have a director and navigator, someone keeping tabs on our thoughts, and to whom we must eventually answer, be it willingly or not. Because the world hurries by so quickly, hurries downhill, help, and everything is irreversible, understand? Irreversible. And how can it be that all the way to the top of the pyramid there are only more people just like us, who tinker hopelessly through days and nights, stitching together the plots of their lives patch after patch; only one fear in us is greater than the fear of being caught, and that's the fear of not being caught, of falling down without a rescuer, all the way down, and there's no bottom.

So we invent limits. So we push at them and hope for a firm hand to hold the leash, even if we choke a little here and there, even if we don't know how to interpret each instruction and order, and even if we're punished for this, still the leash is firmly held, so we won't run into the street, where massive trucks are swarming, ten thousand wheels racing blindly ahead.

So every intelligent man must sleep with a map under the pillow. A folder full of maps, even. And every night, before going to sleep, you kiss your map. You say, thanks, thank you, dear map. Thank you, not for the roads but for the ends of roads. For it's impossible to keep going endlessly. In the end comes the sea. Then, there will be dragons. But it's not a map of the universe. That doesn't end. On and on it goes, and there will always be more to go, and then where will we rest our heads at night?

13

At times he said to himself, I'm a small, frightened animal that lives in a dark forest, with soft fur and sharp teeth (so he said, though actually he was an elementary school teacher). I'm a small, frightened animal in a dense forest, and she, Ariella, is my gentle princess. Soon she will come and save me, will embrace me with her big arms.

Say what you like, but even while fantasizing he's never entirely anchored to the shore of dreams-come-true. He won't allow this under any circumstances. His imaginary life, like his actual life (I won't say his "active" life), is not a bed of roses, or lilies, or violets. Though he strives to keep his actual life trimmed and strong, more than once his imaginary life has grown wild, and this he allows. For example, it's very possible that they'll break up, he and Ariella, after the day comes when they're finally together.

After the first months of joy, when they hardly leave the bed, and when, if she'd go take a bath, he would come in after her and soap up her back, and they would giggle like children, after these months she will decide, let's say, that she's unsatisfied professionally, and she'll go study at the university. He'll encourage her like he always does, will make her coffee when she sits studying for exams at night, they'll talk about Kant (let's say), or maybe optics or the anatomy of the human hand (if she wants to become a doctor or something of that sort), and he'll be embarrassed when she wants to go to student parties. Come on, he'll tell her, everyone's going to say, here's Ariella again with her older boyfriend, what on earth does she see in him, and she'll say, oh, silly, everyone will see how wonderful you are and be jealous, and he'll laugh, and she'll say, no, really, and then they'll go to the party, and when he goes out to the bathroom he'll come back and she'll jump suddenly when she notices him, she'll be sitting and talking with someone her age, and then she'll say, ah, here's Mordechai, he's my boyfriend, and Motti will say, no need for Mordechai, Motti is just fine. And the one she'll be speaking to will say, nice to meet you, and will smile uncomfortably. This one will be a friend of hers from school, he'll start coming over to their place to study, and Motti will see Ariella being swept beyond his reach, and he'll know where to, and even though there's no chance, he'll try to fix it, they'll go on vacation, they'll go to the same place as before even, the place they once were, where they did it for the first time, and she'll sit next to him in the car, they'll be silent sometimes, and sometimes they'll speak like everything's fine, she'll sit next to him (he'll drive) with a blank expression. If she gets a text message, what of it. It's something about work, she'll say (he won't ask). And she'll write a message in reply. Another message comes, another message sent. That blank expression the whole time, and if he tilts the mirror he'll be able to see her blush, blush just a bit, but he won't be able to see the wetness inside her spreading below. He'll see her being swept farther and farther away, and he won't know what to do, perhaps he'll even get angry, but he'll only want her to be happy, he'll struggle for awhile, in the end weaken, and she'll take her things and leave. Again he'll be lost, time will close in around him, stifling and vicious, and he'll wait at night for her to return, she won't, and so another night and then another, and then—it's unavoidable—he'll sit down again in his old place.

And then it's all over, the plots in his head coinciding with the plot of his actual life, where he also sits down next to the wall, cheek cold, and everything comes apart. He gets up restless and wanders around the apartment, starts the kettle going and then turns it off and forgets about it, letting it get cold again, opens and shuts the door of the refrigerator, and so on, until he gets tired enough to fall asleep, or, if not that, then at least to return to his chair so that something else, not a fact, simple and decisive, like all that, will blossom.

But look at him, sitting next to the wall again and apparently crying out to be saved, that is, for something to remove him from his life, but it appears he isn't doing a thing to make this happen, so perhaps he simply deserves this and that's that, no? Perhaps he simply deserves this and that's that.

14

Overall, in life, the possibilities for action are quite numerous. If we are among those people who tend to go out into the street for a walk, and then a man comes toward us on that street, it doesn't matter if we know him or not, if we like him or are revolted by him or even fear him, there is nothing physically preventing him, for instance, from extending a hand in greeting. There is nothing physically preventing us from saying to him, go away you shit, you ugly asshole you. There is nothing that prevents one from being nasty, from insulting, scratching, spitting in his eye. One must, however (that is, one can—there's no obligation to do a thing like this), be kind, it's better for all of us this way, but there's no real obstacle to doing otherwise. There's nothing preventing a man from coming along and saying to us, "Hello, Yechiel!" and we, in turn (even if our name is, for instance, Yechiel), can definitely say to him, sir, you clearly have me confused with someone else. Me, my name is actually Mr. Noam Etzion (though that's not what we're called—maybe someone among us is, that's certain, but certainly not all of us; how confusing it would be if that's what we were all called, and on the other hand, how economical). Afterward, once he's convinced, and we've already turned to walk away, we'll turn our head to him, we'll lock our eyes on his, on the look he's sent us from behind, and we'll do this for only a moment, just enough to sow a doubt in him that will never settle again.

Therefore, simply out of spite for this abundance of possibilities, we intentionally restrict ourselves again and again. Close down the potentialities so they don't get in the way, so we don't get our nose stuck deep in life's permissiveness, deep inside the need to decide, time after time, again. Therefore, even in moments of great indecision, one must keep this in mind: all roads, even the ones that seem widest, spreading out before our eyes, are just a fraction of all the unseen paths we could take. When we complain about the seeming closure, about the lives we'll never have under any circumstances, it's important to remember that freedom lurks around every corner. That liberty, like a giant wave, threatens to sweep us away at any moment. If we only let up, if we lose control, we'd be lost in a sea of action and capitulation with no land in sight.

At difficult moments, therefore, I only want to remind us all not to complain. Our lives are really not so complicated. They're closed up rather well, we put so many limits and barriers in them to narrow the path for ourselves so that we don't get lost (so that we have a character as well).

One need not think about this with contempt. But with gratitude. Even joy. We close life up again and again, and it's possible to break out all at once. Paths have already been blazed for us in thought, and we stroll down them out of habit. But it must be possible to do otherwise. It must be. Otherwise like Motti we'll wander around our lives like a boy around a cat's corpse, poking it with a stick to make it wake up, to make it not wake up, it's not clear what this poking's about, that is, who's keeping him there and who he's punishing, the cat itself or death (certainly not the stick), and who he imagines is lying there with its tongue sticking out and gums withdrawing after death—his father, his mother, the dog waiting for him, still alive, at home? Not himself yet. Himself he hasn't yet imagined dead (or only very obliquely). Maybe no one at all, only this: the cat, death, the death of the cat.

15

Hey man, said Menachem on the telephone, because it was Wednesday, and the time was a little after six.

Hey Menachem, Motti said. How's it going?

Awesome, Menachem said. You feel like maybe catching a movie?

A movie? Motti was surprised, an unjustifiable lump stuck in his throat, because it was Wednesday, and for years now they've gone out in the evening to drink in exactly the same pub, each ordering a half liter for starters (afterward Menachem would continue with other drinks, and joke around with the waitress). What movie? Where? I don't know if that really makes sense for me today.

What are you getting stressed about, you? Menachem laughed. Drop it, just drop it. I thought we'd catch a movie, but we don't have to. Be downstairs in an hour, we'll get a drink.

Yeah, sure. Motti was embarrassed. In an hour downstairs, man.

And an hour later he was indeed downstairs, as usual. Menachem, who was a little early, was already there, having trouble with the baby's car seat, which was securely fastened in front. The son of a bitch won't come off, said Menachem. Wait a bit, I'll be with you in a sec.

Pulled, pushed, and in the end it came loose, the son of a bitch, and Motti got in the car, picking up two pacifiers and a bottle with a colorful nipple from the floor before putting on his seatbelt. They

45

went downtown, drove around for a few minutes and looked for a place to park close by, in the end Menachem squeezed real tight between two cars, dismissed with a scornful snort a little bump that also set off the alarm of the car in front of him, and a moment or two later they were already sitting down in their place and ordering.

So what's with Edna? Motti asked. And how are the kids?

What sweeties! Menachem said enthusiastically. They're my life, they are. I'm fucking crazy about them. Beautiful like their mother, and smarter than their father (a thousand times you could ask him the same questions, a thousand times you'd get the same answers; from Motti's perspective it was definitely reassuring). And what's with you, eh? Let me tell you, until you get yourself one of these kids, you won't understand what this whole stinking life is worth at all. This whole fucking life.

Sat quietly and drank. I almost forgot! (Menachem suddenly announced and sent his hand into his bag.) I got you that movie you wanted.

Man (Motti was happy), where'd you find it? Do you know how long I've been looking for this?

I know, of course I know, Menachem said. Otherwise I wouldn't have tried so hard in the first place.

This is so great (Motti said and caressed the cassette absentmindedly). What, was it hard to find?

Nonsense, Menachem said dismissively. What are friends for, eh?

This is so great (Motti repeated, still caressing). Listen, I owe you.

Nonsense, Menachem said, and hello hello, he said to the waitress passing by their table, be a sweetheart and bring two more like this to me and my brother here, will you? What an ass on that one (he said to Motti when the waitress moved away from their table, sending a long look after her). Why won't you talk to her, maybe get something out of it, eh?

I don't think so, Motti said.

Why overthink it? Menachem wondered (and justly, to a not-insignificant extent). I'm telling you, looks to me that since I got married there's only more pussy in the world. A man could wander around all day with sore balls just from looking, and you, it's not like you already have someone to unwind with, right? Or do you have someone you're not telling your brother about? Don't get me wrong, okay? You're a stand-up guy, you know I'm fucking crazy about you, but sometimes I look at you and say, I swear on my mother, once again the Holy-One-Blessed-is-He gave nuts to someone without teeth (and again he laughed; at his own wit). Just say the word and I'll get that waitress's telephone number. (She now returned to the table with two glasses. Thanks, sweetie, Menachem said to her, and she smiled.) So, lucky for you that you teach elementary, huh? Menachem laughed. Think if you were teaching high school, what sore balls, huh? All day those young girls around, I swear on my mother, if back then you would have told me that someday I'd want them even more than I did then, I would have laughed in your face.

Motti shifted in place uncomfortably.

My God, Menachem said, just don't go getting all offended, huh? Listen, my man, Menachem continues and pats his shoulder, you're so sensitive, you know I'm crazy about you.

16

Got back home and watched the movie. Good movie. And then watched the credits, of course. And then sat a bit facing the screen. Then watched the news. Why, he too lives in this country. Harsh scenes shown, one must assume. The newscaster lowered his eyes and even spoke in a dramatic voice. Motti himself was upset, it's only natural. Someone needs to do something, it's truly necessary, but who and what, this is not entirely clear.

Yes, the world troubles him, make no mistake. The items on the news trouble him, the articles in the papers. The fighting voices that echo in the stairwell trouble him when Mickey and Sigal (neighbors of his, I swear it's them) start up again, and again the yells rise up and sometimes the sound of a smack, too, and then another sort of ambiguous groan, and crying. But what should he do, Motti—learn how to hit, buy a club and brass knuckles, wear a ski mask and go out into the night to take revenge? What is he, a little kid? Come what may, no brass knuckles will enter this book. Furthermore, even the most evil bastards, he knows, once had someone who loved them, who saw in them something beautiful. And if not, there's just one more reason to feel sorry for them. Maybe not to let them off the hook, to forgive, but certainly to feel sorry for them.

And anyway, what kind of stupidity is it to think we can simply cover our face and have no one recognize us! It's impossible to deceive dogs this way, for example, and this thought, of hiding and concealing and evading, it begins with our loyalty to the eye, to vision. We take from this a subtle pleasure—the spirit floats on waves of light as if we had no part in the vulgar matter! Only the eye has this quality (even hearing—from a physiological perspective, that is, as far as biological receptors are involved—is a type of touching). And so we turn our gaze away from the things that smell and the bristly hairs on the back of our hand, from our trembling and pulsing internal organs, and so we turn our faces away, turn our backs on our excretions, how vulgar. Again and again we encounter these things with almost pornographic wonder, the diluted insult that comes with being reminded of the corporeal creatures that we are, and a bit of fear in it too (excretions are emissaries of our inner body to the world of the eye—we are detectives always on the watch for fecal blood).

17

Since morning, because a strike had been announced, Motti wandered restlessly around his apartment. From time to time voices of children playing rose up from the street, and he, who had his fill of children each day at work, sat down to watch television but didn't find it interesting, decided to use the time to grade exams, but this didn't fill up more than a half hour, tried to read a book but the words got away from him. Thought it was noon already and decided to sit down to eat, maybe make an omelet, even though he wasn't hungry at all, but the clock on the oven instructed him that it wasn't even ten A.M. Didn't want to pick up the phone to call anyone, and in any case who did he have to talk to, everyone's at work, and who is this everyone after all, and in any case there wasn't anything pressing he had to say. Tried listening to records, but the old music annoyed him for being old, whereas the new music annoyed him for being unfamiliar. Twice called for the time, went to the video store and rented a movie, but didn't feel like actually watching it, and anyway who sits down to watch a movie in the middle of the day. When he thought to take Laika out again for a walk she just opened a sleepy eye at him and remained lying on the armchair in the living room. He always complains that he has no free time, and believes that if he had some he might finally sit down to do something substantive, something with meaning, learn to play an instrument or write a book, maybe start exercising, but who's he kidding (plus, why bother on the day of a strike? it might end tomorrow), he doesn't even feel like sorting the weekend newspapers, doesn't even feel like collecting them and throwing them in the garbage. They say that in the military prison there are inmates who sculpt chewed-up bread, how disgusting. It's possible to start sculpting with clay, with plaster, with papier-mâché, with processed leather, with bonsai trees, with aluminum foil, with mixed media, only all of his artistic experiments from the past (that is to say, from childhood) failed because he gave up. He knew that it was a mistake, and yet each time he expected that he would manage to create something utterly without blemish, something complete in itself—but again and again his hopes were dashed (and this is one of the many differences between us: I believe that a creation must bear the scars of its creation).

Whoever might see Motti wandering around like this in his apartment might think of a butterfly or an insect imprisoned in a transparent case: fluttering back and forth. But how can one escape from inside time? You should be ashamed of yourself, he reprimands himself. In Africa people search for food for their dying children, and you, since you have nothing to do with yourself, you complain.

One day, he says to himself, someone will come (he doesn't say *Ariella*, even though deep in his heart he believes that one day, if he only keeps himself strong, it will indeed be her) and remove you from yourself like a banana from its blackened peel.

Eventually he did convince Laika to go out for a walk. The two of them trudged on indifferently. Laika sniffed and he stared into space. Walked the length of the block, sometimes in the shade and sometimes in the sun, according to the caprice of municipal architects and landscapers. His thinking roamed to uninteresting places, and when they turned right on one of the streets he saw a woman from far away, walking ahead of him, for a moment his mind mocked him and he thought, here is the grown-up Ariella, and he hurried after her, loyal Laika following in his tracks, and she, who heard his steps from behind, even before he could consider placing a hand on her shoulder, a thing he wouldn't do, turned around smiling. Oh, excuse me, he said, I thought you were someone else. What a coincidence! she laughed. I really am someone else!

Another moment he stood there, maybe even with his mouth open. There are really great responses to that sentence, amazing comebacks, but they only show up after the fact. She smiled again, turned, and walked away. Motti and Laika also turned around and returned home. No one was waiting in the stairwell (and why would someone be waiting?), and the time was only three in the afternoon. Even though he wasn't hungry at all, he prepared a salad and a bit of rice with vegetables: a TV dinner. This was a very balanced meal, and he ate every last bite, albeit without appetite, almost out of obligation. Indeed, the body needs all sorts of things, carbohydrates and proteins and minerals and a soft touch now and then, and so forth, but the mind is like a child, it eats almost only sugar. This is a physiological fact.

18

Maybe, when they really get to know each other, Motti will discover that she's one of those cheerful women, always happy, but not out of ignorance or blindness, rather out of a good and proper view of the world, out of the hope—the belief—that we always have the ability to fix things, and that every day there is someone out there who is actually doing it, even though not everyone sees and these things aren't reported by the media. During the day she'll be in pants and a comfortable shirt, her hair either gathered up or loose, all over the place, she'll walk with a big bag and in it, let's say, cigarettes and a lighter and a telephone for calling him when she wants to hear his voice, and also a bag of food for stray dogs or street cats. She'll walk around and hum pleasant melodies as if absentminded, giving passersby a kind expression, everything she does she'll do out of casual happiness. Perhaps that's how she'll dress, and perhaps the contents of her bag will indeed be as imagined (cigarettes and food for dogs, etc.), but her mood, he'll discover once he gets to know her better, isn't quite as he presumed: she'll be a little morose and pensive, the evils of the world will weigh heavily on her until she can't bear it anymore, but she'll go on fighting for everything worth fighting for regardless. Almost to the point of exhaustion, every day. And only at night, when they'll rest in bed together, she'll suddenly let go. Motti, she'll say to him, my Mordechai, sometimes I think that only you give me the strength to carry on, and he'll say, nonsense, my beauty. I just . . . I'm not the issue here. It's all you, all of it.

But deep inside he'll smile and hope that it's nevertheless true.

And if that's how she'll be, maybe when they're together her hairstyle won't be as described above, but always smartly pulled back, to be let down only at home in the evening. Held tight in a rubber band, lest the world's stench get into in it. Everyone who meets her will say, Ariella is a tough woman. Good but tough as nails, you won't find a drop of gentleness in her. Only Motti will know the truth, that she has another side entirely, and it's kept just for him and no one else. Okay, okay, maybe it's not kept just for him, but only in his presence, when he holds her at night, is she free, does she let go, breathe deeply, laugh when he jokes tenderly.

Maybe she'll be, let's say, a social worker, deadly serious. She'll run some center for abused girls, she'll guide them with a firm hand, she'll give them exactly what they need, structure and clear rules, but if one of them breaks down sobbing, Ariella will hug and calm them down like no one else. A reinforced wall, that one. She won't let anyone harm the girls, not difficult parents, not boyfriends who are bad influences. And once every few weeks, maybe even every Friday evening, one of the girls will come over to Motti and Ariella's place. Their own foster child, a tough life she's had, and Ariella will make her into an artist or a concert pianist, and

they'll collect newspaper clippings of deeply sympathetic reviews and in-depth interviews, and the foster child will say in
them, I owe everything to that woman, her name is Ariella, she
believed in me when no one else would. The girl will be like their
daughter when she grows up, and if they move, withered, to an
old-folks home on the edge of town, that girl (who will of course
already be grown up by then) will come to visit with her family, because she won't be ungrateful, she'll know that one should
never deny an obligation, and that debts must be repaid, and
with love too, maybe even primarily with love. She also won't be
ashamed of her past. She'll say to her spouse, to their children
(maybe there will even be grandchildren), look, this is Ariella
and this is Motti, without them none of this would have happened, and who knows what would have happened to me otherwise, maybe I'd be dead already if the two of them hadn't gotten
me out the way they did. Her own children will already be pulling at her dress or her shirt or whatever she'll wear then (there's
nothing to get mad about, they're children, their patience is
short), and they'll ask to go home, and he and Ariella will walk
the whole family to her car (if the two of them can still walk,
aging is a cruel thing after all). Then they'll return to their room
and he'll put the kettle on and hand in hand they'll sit down, let's
say, to watch television.

And maybe, thinks Motti, maybe her hair won't be tied up like
that in the first place. Maybe she'll have a long braid, a thick, smooth
one that will rest lazily on her back. A dark braid that she'll nurture
as long as the two of them are still relatively young. At night she'll
brush her hair in long strokes, every morning he'll braid it for her

beautifully. From time to time perhaps she'll be lazy, she'll keep the braid up and get into bed like that, to sleep, and if they make love then, he could, with the braid, c'mon, really, he could do what he could do. There are some things that we don't have to know.

19

He wanted their first time to be very special, and sometimes thought about a regular sort of special, a routine special, like satin sheets and flower petals that a woman from room service could scatter around for twenty shekels an hour, without benefits, without any employer contributions to her retirement fund.

Sometimes he thought otherwise. Thought about a special that would be truly unique, the two of them in a moment of passion in the stockroom of the houseware or clothing store that Ariella will maybe be working at one day (just a student job, only a temporary job, bigger things than this will still await her), and each thing that pokes one of them in the butt will be special, every strange contortion forced upon them by a surprising caprice of architecture, every sharp metal corner that scratches his or her bare leg (even a knock on the head from a ceiling that slopes downward toward the back wall).

And then, sometimes he thought about special in a car. The two of them will go on a vacation to the mountains, the two of them know what's coming and look forward to this first, exciting act of love, many more of which are to come, even that same night. And then, on the side of the road, the carburetor will die. The car will get stuck, but they won't call to get towed. They'll take out a thermos from the bag they packed in advance, sit on the side of the road and watch the passing cars. And talk about life. She'll say, it's funny how we were neighbors once, and I looked at you like that on the stairs, and he'll say, funny, right. And then he'll be quiet for a moment, and say, you know, I already had a feeling back then that one day we'd be together. She'll laugh. What, really? And he'll say, of course. She'll laugh again, and then she'll understand that he meant it seriously, she'll smile and hug him. So they'll sit another moment in silence, and then she'll tremble. Are you cold (he'll ask)? And she'll just nod. They'll get inside the car. And she, as if unintentionally, will reach her right hand out to his pants. And free him (his member, I mean) from there. His breath will immediately halt, and then he'll expel the air with a loud, heavy sigh. And she'll take off her pants, take off her underwear too, and sit down on him slowly. By the wandering glow of the lights on the car's ceiling, on its seats, on their bodies, on her face that will be raised up with eyes closed, on her hair that will be spread out like a curtain over his likewise closed eyes, on her breasts that will be freed from her shirt whose buttons will be undone, on his tongue, on the hands that will embrace, on the mouths that will open, the tongues that will reach places you couldn't fathom, the hungry fingers, the body rising and falling, the air that will escape through lips wide open, the moan, the moans, the moan.

Never had he come like that. Only that one time: as if a herd of horses were racing down his whole body, thundering the length of the arms and legs, a thousand manes wild in the wind, everything throbbing in his stomach and the tips of his fingers, and all the mighty horses galloping down the full length of his body as if he's a vast plain with grass that bends blithely in the wind, all of them galloping until they exit from him in a single, sustained rumble. And the breath is caught in his throat, almost shrieking. As if his soul is only barely kept inside. As if it had already started leaving, most of it already out, and only the tip of its tail caught on something, and then all of it gets pulled back inside again, a second wave of pleasure that will be almost too great to contain.

Or they'll arrive at the inn. Like an experienced, seasoned married couple they will unpack their bags, they'll place their folded clothes properly in the closets, put on water for coffee, consider what to eat that evening.

And they'll return excited from dinner, the two of them will already know what's about to happen for the first time. He'll wait in their shared bed and look at the light leaking from the milky glass of the bathroom window, what is she doing in there for so long, and then she'll come out in a nightgown that will spill like water over her body (which will be naked under it, I mean under the nightgown), and she'll get into bed. There will be absolute darkness, outside just crickets and a distant jackal, and like the jackal he too will only want to howl, to let out everything rising inside him after so many years of waiting. Her fingers will caress his face, afterward his chest, afterward further down than this. And then, when he can't get it up, she'll take it in her hand (I mean his sexual organ) like a baby chick and breathe on it to arouse him. Years he waited, it's understandable that now he's too excited. They'll lie in bed, and she'll smile at him that way for the first time, and his two hands will spread her legs which perhaps will still be a little chubby, behind her knees will be drops of warm perspiration, and then he'll enter her slowly and sweetly, and this is how they'll do it, she'll hug him and be happy even though maybe he'll finish too quickly, because what difference does it make, an entire lifetime of love still awaits them.

Will she scream when she comes? Will she only gasp for air? Maybe she'll just sigh with a voice so faint it will barely be heard, but he will listen, will know that he brought her this pleasure.

20

In the end they'll be together forever, Motti thinks while the lights of nighttime cars outline his shadow in the room, on the wall against which he's placed his left cheek, etc.

But this "forever," what does it mean? Will they be together until the very end, that is, in the same moment close their eyes and take leave of the world? Maybe there will be a terminal disease. And it will attack Ariella. They'll fight it together, they'll spend all their savings, longing to draw out each remaining moment of life, just another week to hold hands, another month. And together they'll return in the end from the hospital, the diagnosis will be clear—from now on, only pain and suffering, but the end is known. Therefore they'll put on a disc of beautiful music, and together they'll get into bed and swallow a jar of pills, and nothing will ever get between Ariella and him again, they'll lay so close, and between them only the jar, only the fumes from the exhaust, only the plastic bag that will cover their faces. Perhaps they'll even smile in the end, fixing the other with a look overflowing with acceptance and beauty, each of them, deep in their hearts, hoping nevertheless to die first, so as not to live even a moment alone, so as not to see the eyes opposite theirs glaze over, the tongue hanging out. So as not to hear the last breath.

First Ariella will object. This is for certain. She'll say, I don't want you to die with me too. I want you to remain, to be filled with joy, to fall in love again, to remember or forget me, to do whatever is best for you. And he'll say, no. No. Years before you knew who I was at all, I thought about you. About our life together. I also thought about this moment. I decided long ago, you are my life, and without you I have nothing. Time and again they'll have this very conversation, different versions. And when she understands that there's no way to convince him, understands that there is no other possibility, that she can't dissuade him, she'll hold his hand tightly and smile a sad smile, maybe the two of them will cry, and then he'll go to the kitchen and make her an omelet like she loves, and she'll try to eat, but the nausea, the nausea. In the days after this she will be brave and courageous, never again will they travel silently to the oncology ward, they'll just finish, let's say, reading a few books they planned to read but hadn't gotten to, just finish accumulating enough pills, and that's all, off to bed.

And if he's the sick one, if his body is scanned magnetically in a search for some out of control, metastasizing intruder, if a forehead strap is wrapped around his head, packed with electrodes and conductive wires, adorning him like laurel leaves? They'll slide him inside like a conqueror, into the guts of the rattling machine. Two weeks after this, no more, already the funeral. And people will cry and people will restrain themselves, and people will say, oh, oh, such a good man he was, why was he taken oh why. And she'll stand among them with a secret hidden behind her expression. And before this the two of them will talk about everything, they'll talk all about his approaching death—not like us, who look away from others' coming deaths as though they were dog shit.

And if he dies before this in a car crash, God forbid, if he's cut apart and all his foul-smelling physiological secrets that were hidden until then behind his skin are spilled out, Ariella will be there to hold his hand while his pulse fades, his life running out with the beating of his treacherous heart, which until now was needed to live but now at last has revealed its true plan, to pump out all his blood, to push it out of his gaping wound so he'll cease, be done, so little Motti will die like this on the road, and from a distance the sound of sirens is heard, but he only barely hears it, and every second is already so precious, every second is like a rare piece of jewelry that Ariella will wear for the rest of her life, the few years that remain to her, and she'll grope those forlorn beads of memory when she rolls over in her bed at night. (Alone, he hopes. For at least a few years it will still only be her, and even afterward some wound will remain, a sliver of longing, a gaping biographical hole, some sorrow.)

21

Look at this, so many possibilities one can fabricate without committing to any actual story.

The body of the plot is full of holes like a fisherman's net or an old stocking, and as with the net, it gathers up, without discretion, miscellaneous thoughts and meaningless fantasies and so forth. But that's how we speak through the pages of a book, so why hide it? On the contrary. Apart from whatever glance God—if there is such a thing—might throw us from time to time, there isn't a lot of meaning to the things we do when we're all alone. The only acts that have any salient existence are those done in company. That being the case, I would even suggest we meet up for coffee or something, but ordinarily I'm not a particularly good conversationalist. Quite the opposite. Unremittingly quiet or else babbling on—not to mention that since quitting smoking I don't know what you're supposed to do with your hands when talking.

22

But a day later, when Motti returned from work, Ariella was waiting there on the stairs, drumming on her backpack and chewing gum.

My mom still isn't home, she said to him. Can I wait at your place?

I, I, Motti said, his heart pounding. I myself am not going inside, actually. I just dropped by . . . dropped by to . . . I have, I really have to go, I just dropped by.

He fled down the stairs as if wolves were nipping at his heels, and hid among the bushes in the backyard for perhaps an hour and a half, until her mom returned. Only then did he go up cautiously, quickly drink a glass of water, peek through the peephole to see that no one was standing in the stairwell, put Laika on her leash, and out together to walk the streets.

And so, has your opinion of him changed, now that it's been made perfectly clear that she's just a kid? It's important to remember that he still hasn't done a thing. Won't, either. Why, she's just a child, why, that's disgusting, the very thought of touching her like that disgusts him, no matter how much he wants to touch her when she grows up, when they're in love.

As proof, even if he was asked for whatever reason to describe her to someone, he wouldn't have any problem describing her quite well (indeed, he's observed her for hours, a minute here, a minute there, from the window or through the peephole in his front door), but he doesn't know how she smells, what smell she has, he's never gotten sufficiently close to her. Likewise, and this maybe even more important still, he would without any doubt skip over in his description the secondary sexual characteristics that are even now beginning to be hinted at by her body. He'd skip her ass, which will grow rounder in future, and he wouldn't even think about the first signs of her breasts, already showing. Also not about what there is between her legs, even though in his fantasies this keeps him very busy, because how can this be, how can a person have an opening that another person can enter?

And not only will he skip these descriptions. Also the thoughts.

And this even though he watches her for hours and wonders what she'll be like when she grows up.

Will she grow to be tall and skinny like a shoot? Skinny, skinny, another moment and the wind will carry her away, even though she walks so determinedly against it, walking up some street against the wind, lowering her head decisively. Her cheekbones will almost cut the flesh of her cheeks, they'll protrude that much, but they won't look harsh and cruel. Just the opposite. Delicate. With straight hair she'll walk like that, in a T-shirt a little too big for her, her eyes light green now, with a hint of honey, giving them depth. Forest green, those eyes, rich, you can just drown in them. Or the opposite, she'll almost be pudgy, sturdy, with round and heavy breasts, smiling. At night she'll rest her head on his chest and absentmindedly caress him as they watch the TV. And he in return, teasing her—just as she plays with his chest hair, so he plays with her breasts. Places a hand there and swings them back and forth (this isn't sexual, it's a lover's joke), and so they laugh together, her and him, a laugh of deep recognition. After they calm down, and the laughter subsides, he'll say to her, my love, I love you more than anything. I love your hands more than anything, your legs, your tummy, the lines of your face, your spleen, the toes on your feet, your nails, your eyelashes, this beauty mark, that beauty mark, and this one as well, your voice, the way you move, your fantasies, your beautiful thoughts, your pupils, your nostrils, the hairs in your nostrils (and she'll protest, I have absolutely no hairs in my nostrils!—he'll correct himself, the nonhairs in your nostrils, but the hairs in your ears I just adore! and she'll protest, and he'll continue), I love your neck more than anything, your cute ass, your shins, your knees, keep going? The back of your knees, elbows, shoulders, your boobs, your little belly button (she'll say, what, you don't love my, you know, vagina? and he'll say, I love it, just love it), your earlobes, the nape of your neck, behind your ears, your tongue, your teeth, your forehead, your cheeks, your gums. I love to see your hair more than anything. More than anything I love to see it shoot off your shoulders like little flames, like a bonfire. And she'll say in a sweet voice, what's burning? He'll say, my heart, dear, and laugh deeply, as though belittling the beautiful things that he himself just said.

And if fate—of all things—laughs at him, and they actually don't meet again when she's grown up, without even knowing, some door will close in him that was open only for her. This he's already mourned, in the very moment he thought of it: that with her he could be a man who he could never be without her. Not a better man, not necessarily, but nevertheless a different man, and if nothing out of all the things he's now thought up will ever be, then this man too will never come to be, and already now he mourns his ongoing departure (mourns the thoughts he won't think when she won't be there, the jokes that won't come to him, even the small acts of cruelty that in her presence are liable to break loose inside him and who knows where they'll blossom now, if at all).

23

And if I may, like officers in the army are so fond of doing, offer a personal example, I'll point out only the diamonds that glittered at me years ago, as a boy, on the way back from Friday night dinner at Grandma's. Giant diamonds and chandeliers sparkling that I spotted from a distance, on the ceiling of some wonderful house that you could see from the road for a moment, through the car window, and they stayed with me so many years, until two or three months ago I actually went there, to the actual place, to someone's Bar Mitzvah celebration. And instantly all of them, all the diamonds and such, transformed into neon lights (even though in my memory there still remains something of all the marvelous radiance, and this paragraph is proof).

And this, now, is the question: Is it possible to accuse Motti of clinging to his diamonds in this way? That he avoids (as a way of life, properly speaking) ever standing in the hall and looking upward, negating his memory, feeling some dim contempt for anyone who believes there are really diamonds like that in the world?

It's clear that Motti must be accused of something. And there is certainly something to accuse him of. The question is if it's this. Which is one of the central questions of this book, even if not one of the more interesting ones in it. We have to ask if the freedom he's suckling at is real, valid. And then, if there's anything we can learn from his behavior. Or is it just the opposite, is it that you actually need to get dirty in the world, to immerse yourself in the neon light of the actual, in disappointment, in trudging forward and then sprinting ahead all of a sudden, through doors slammed shut.

24

(And he's wrong, that much is clear. There's no comfort inside one's head. Not like there is in one body with another, in that warmth, in the touch.)

25

You've certainly already noticed that I haven't in any way empha-
sized the idea of Ariella's innocence, her actual childhood, her
childish innocence, etc. Moreover: I almost haven't talked about
her at all. About her personality, her likes and dislikes. She's here
most of the time as a sort of tabula rasa, a potentiality upon which
it's possible to hang anything. And it's this way not only for literary reasons, but also because I don't believe in innocence, that is,
in discussions about it, that is, in those speaking about it. Maybe
only Patti Smith. Or maybe not even her. If there's any innocence
at all, it comes out of choice and hard work. And I don't say this
to be a smart ass. Not at all. Only in order to be understood. Because anything else would be overblown. Really too much. Because
storytelling itself, this craft, well, it's a very dubious enterprise. To
sit and invent things that never were for others to sit and strain to
believe in them for a moment, maybe to learn from them, maybe
to get emotional. So it's hard for me to commit to a story. To this
suspicious craft. To devote myself to it, to a single, closed plot, to its
characters. If I may be allowed to say so (and certainly I may, this is
my book), it's just like in life, in life too it's hard sometimes to devote oneself to something without reservation, to touch skin with

our own skin, with everything that will be lost to us eventually, will be lost to us in death or even before. On the other hand (again, like in life, sorry), what's all this worth if we don't give in and hug and love and so on? There's something to be said for distancing ourselves, true, but the rewards are very bitter. And I already know how all this will end, how my characters will end up and the book as a whole (I even budgeted its word count). Hence these games of distancing and drawing near, again and again: with all due respect, I think it's up to my characters to make the effort and come closer to me. Then we'll see. In American movies they say this attitude also works with women. But American movies, you know.

26

But nevertheless, something happens.

So out they went, drinking again.

Again Menachem drank a bit too much, drank till he became rude; he pressured the waitress to be nice to Motti, who sat there in despair, and to give him her telephone number—while Motti sat there reserved—and maybe go out and have a drink with them later, when her shift was over. She gave Motti a friendly smile, to Menachem her smile was less friendly and she declined as she always did (she wanted to go home too, to study for her test; she wants to be a veterinarian, to take care of hurt and abandoned animals; after doing it for years, she'll grow a little duller, she'll nurse a profound hostility toward dog owners who just can't wait to put to sleep or give away the pets who so adore them, and an even greater hostility toward those who refuse to spay and neuter: "We want her to experience the joy of giving birth, and for the children to enjoy it too, that connection with nature, there's nothing like it," they say, and they don't know what they're saying, don't know about the puppies crowding the cages of shelters and pounds, soon put to death or dying of their own accord; and she too, when she's already a district vet, she'll start being a little too free with the syringe, in the evening she'll go home just wanting to forget it all, put her feet up on the coffee table and sigh; her own dog will put its head on her knees, looking at her expectantly, and she'll stroke her—the dog—absentmindedly and think of suffering).

Then they went out again, and Menachem said, cut the crap, I'm fine, come on, I'll give you a ride home.

So in they got, fastened their seatbelts, and started to drive. And then that dull thud (I didn't see where she came from, I didn't see her, Menachem said over and over, like he was possessed or something), and the crowd collecting after they got out of the car, the police lights, the muttering, the shouts, even the great astonishment, for up till now it was the persistence of life that had surprised Menachem. When his children were small he would wake in a panic from bad dreams and hurry to their room to check whether they were still breathing or if they'd died in their sleep, nothing to it, like a spark shining brightly, briefly, then going out completely and that's that. Not that it was always easy with them, no, mostly he didn't know what to do with them, with the kids and Edna, alive and his and they're all together, but the thought of losing them, that they wouldn't be there anymore (that there would no longer be any possibility of being together, whether this possibility was taken advantage of or not), that was something he couldn't conceive of.

So he hurried to their room at night again and again, and was astonished every time to see how life was preserved, how this stubborn thread continued, this metabolism, these breaths. And now, one little blow—and that was it. Sarah Rosenthal's soul departed in an instant, assuming she had one in the first place (assuming we all do, whether fictional or not). What could Menachem do? Around him shouts and flashing lights, cries of Mister, Mister, and him in the middle of it all, going back to the car and sitting down in the passenger seat, he wants to keep his distance from the steering wheel, his head in his hands, his nose and then his hands full of snot, moaning like a monkey, like a miserable animal, and Motti by the open car door, still standing. Oh God oh God (he moans), what have I done, Motti, what have I done, I swear I never saw her, oh God, Edna's going to kill me, what am I going to do now.

Dear Dad (Menachem's son might have written to him had he gone to jail) please by me a horse

Mom misses you a lot and she crys all the time she gets angri with us but we know its onliey becos she misses you and its hard for her and we miss you too and we want to come and visit you soon

Yours with love your son Avi

So weak he suddenly became, Menachem.

Edna's going to kill me, he said. My kids will grow up without a father, what will I tell them. This is my third offence, they'll fuck me over in court.

And when the paramedic asked, is someone here with her, Motti said, yes, we are. Then the paramedic said, we're going to such-and-such hospital; they put her in the trauma ward, and there was an elderly man who stroked his stomach and moaned loudly Mama Mama, and to anyone willing to listen he said, two days already I haven't had a bowel movement, two days already I haven't had a bowel movement, and he stroked the tubes inserted into his nostrils and said, it's for the asthma I've been suffering from for fifteen years now, and Motti looked at him and looked at the group of people, a family, standing nearby around the bed of someone else, a woman, and there too there was an elderly man with an expressionless face, and next to him his sons and his daughter in a babble of cell phones ("The doctors say that Mom won't . . ."), and a Filipina caregiver, also standing next to the bed and weeping bitterly; then Sarah's family arrived as well, and somebody asked, who's the driver who hit her? And Menachem said nothing, just sat there trembling weakly, and Motti stood up and said, it's me, I'm the driver. Menachem didn't even look up. And next to them stood Sarah Rosenthal's husband, and her children stood there too, and Motti in the middle of it all stood facing them and said, I'm the driver. Then the fist and the cracked eye socket. They took care of Motti, too. Then the police arrived, and from there to the lock-up, and just as everyone in the hospital had proclaimed their afflictions, so in the lockup everyone proclaimed their innocence, everyone, that is, but Motti. And after a few days or weeks in court, even though it was a first offence, the judge came down on him hard, five years inside, he said. He came down hard both because it was a grave offence and because by then Sarah Rosenthal was dead, and also because his stomach hurt a lot—his daughter had pierced her eyebrow, which made him very angry (and maybe that's why his stomach hurt), and even though Menachem, sitting in the public gallery, flinched—afterward he said, I owe you, brother, man, oh boy do I owe you—Motti didn't even blink, five years, so what, what was that but five years in which he wouldn't have to struggle, which he wouldn't have to struggle to fill up now, until Ariella.

27

So, did he do this in order to finally invert their balance of power? Suddenly the power is in Motti's hands, and the debt will flip, as will everything. But this is a dubious thesis at best, because you can't invert power structures just like that. If only the consequences had occurred to Motti, the great break in the order of things as they should be—even as they must be—perhaps he would have decided differently. But none of this occurred to him, just a desire to be restrained, a desire to contribute (to take a part of the blame, one might add), and without thinking about it he gave in to these desires. Now: guilt proclaimed, blessed routine, just one decision and everything is already out of his hands. A few years out of his hands. He'll sit in his cell like he did in the hallway, in a doorway, waiting calmly, stubborn in a freedom born from borders now solidified, from the closing of doors, from necessarily diminishing choices. And the years ahead will indeed wait, everything will settle, shrink, recede, just as it should.

SECOND

IN BETWEEN

Now we may describe these cases by saying that we have certain sensations not referring to objects. The phrase "not referring to objects" introduces a grammatical distinction. If in characterizing such sensations we use verbs like "fearing," "longing," etc., these verbs will be intransitive; "I fear" will be analogous to "I cry." We may cry about something, but what we cry about is not a constituent of the process of crying; that is to say, we could describe all that happens when we cry without mentioning what we are crying about.

—Ludwig Wittgenstein, *The Blue Book*

28

It's hard to follow stories to their end. Especially when they don't actually take place. As though someone took a small hammer and struck a sheet of glass. The center of the break is obvious to the eye, and from it the fracture's lines run and branch out again and again, and at each juncture the paths grow more and more narrow (they're no less crooked, nor do the number of branches decrease). It's hard to follow them, and anyway, what kind of idiot strikes a sheet of glass like that? Here, for example, is a story in which Motti and Ariella run into each other on May 14th a few years from now: They met one day at a convenience store, it was entirely by chance, in the evening they went to a Chinese or an Italian or a French restaurant or for falafel, they ordered dessert or didn't order dessert, and the dessert reminded her of something or pleased her or, let's say, ruined her diet and at night they returned (let's say) to his apartment, and they made love or just had sex, and Motti came too fast or didn't come too fast, and in the morning, if she stayed until the morning, she put on a white or pink or striped shirt with buttons or without, and she got pregnant or didn't get pregnant, and they were together forever or not, and she became a veterinarian or a librarian or an unemployed interior decorator or a cosmonaut or a surveyor, and each and every day they did something or other.

There, I wrote everything in a hundred and fifty words, even less, but where does love enter into this condensed story, where does Motti's great longing come in, where is the burning passion, the desire to visualize, the urge to realize, the fear, the sweetness?

Overall it would have been better not to write this chapter. Nevertheless, I did.

29

She's had it, Edna has, up to here (she indicates with her hand a bit above eye level). She needs to clean up after him like he's a little boy. If not for the children, she swears she would just leave for good (she says this out of anger; she actually has it good with Menachem most of the time. She loves him).

So be it with the tab at the store (would it kill you to take a wallet when you leave the house, she asks him sometimes in jest and sometimes in real anger, because by now it's getting unpleasant for her too, dealing with that *fellow*—which is, in refined Hebrew, the code word for Arab—who almost begs her each time to talk to Menachem already, to tell him that this is impossible, for years now they've refused to put anything more on the tab, it throws off their books and makes for big trouble with the suppliers and income tax people). So be it. And so be it too, this irresponsibility of his, like a child who promises he'll take care of it and forgets. And so be it too his outings to the city, when they got married she already knew she wouldn't ask him to give this up, bitterness would just build up in him, so why not, let him go out with his friends and enjoy himself, he's a good father and a good husband after all, and even if he has a big mouth out there, she knows which bed he returns to at night (and things are still good between them there, thank God, no complaints).

He almost killed you, that friend of yours (she yells at him). Almost killed you and ran over a poor woman, and now you bring home his dog? Tell me, what's your problem?

What do you want me to do with her, Menachem says in his defense. He's my friend, c'mon. I owe him.

I don't care what you'll do with her, Edna is still angry. Give her to the Humane Society, for all I care.

I can't do a thing like that, Menachem says. C'mon, look how the kids . . .

How the kids, how the kids, Edna is raising her voice. And who'll take her out? You? The kids? And the fur everywhere, who'll clean it up, tell me, who. Everything will fall on me again, Menachem. And I've had it up to here. Up to here, are you listening?

And Laika, standing reluctantly behind Menachem, shrinks at the sound of this shouting.

I'm not mad at you, good dog, Edna says, almost still screaming, but only out of the inertia. C'mon, come inside, both of you.

How could I not take her? Menachem asks as he enters the hallway and drags Laika behind him. Look at her eyes, this dog. Beautiful like your eyes on the day we met (and he slaps her, Edna, on the butt).

You, you . . . ugh, Edna laughs and kneels next to Laika, to pet her.

C'mon, Menachem says, I told you it would be okay. You know I'm fucking crazy about you.

30

And in the house of Sarah Rosenthal, darkness. Her picture on the bureau in the living room (from a time when she was still alive, of course), with her own particular smile, her own particular teeth, her own particular hair, her own particular ears, her own particular chin.

Darkness descended, but no one sitting around got up to turn on the light.

Okay, okay. Not really darkness. When the day began to dim someone got up and turned on the lights, with all the associated unpleasantness, because how can this be, she's dead, and in her home people sit, get up, talk, eat, use electricity. As time passes they will turn on lights without this discomfort, without feeling that something here isn't right (apart from her absence), without looking around with the thought that there's some protocol to death, an order to mourning that one must obey, an attentive force in the blind universe that truly cares if you turn on or don't turn on a light and laugh or don't laugh, fall asleep at night or toss and turn in bed, cry or moan and blow your nose hard.

And Motti is in a cell. To his right a wall and to his left a wall, in front of him a wall (and a door), and behind him a wall, above him and below him only time. Presses an ear to the wall (no voice from the other side) and imagines. True, it's possible to argue that this is unproductive, even pathetic, him and his folded-up life, but he's so free in a way, even in his cell in a prison he's so free, one can only be jealous of this, and even though his actual life is pushed up like this against the wall, the other lives he imagines and remembers are quite numerous, more numerous than usual, even, and there is freedom in this too, and as the years accumulate, when at last time is mainly something stretching out behind us, what does it actually matter what we truly lived and what we only remember living?

In the corridor a bunch of keys jingle. Two prison guards are walking by. "Listen," says one of them, we'll call him Guard A, to his companion, "Listen, I don't understand all this bellyaching with kids today. They sent me a social worker, can you believe that? A social worker. And for what? For what, I ask you. What dad alive doesn't give a little slap here and there, isn't that how it is? Spare the rod, spoil the child, I say. And what, didn't my own parents lower the boom on me from time to time? They lowered it, you bet they lowered it. And it made a better man out of me, let me tell you. I can't pretend I remember every slap, whatever it was for—but so what? I don't remember, but all in all they're good people, I'm telling you. They're good people, my parents. I also turned out—knock on wood—okay. Why should I remember every slap, whatever it was for? So I don't remember. So what. And let me tell you, it's given me the upper hand in life. It's given me the upper hand."

"It's given you a hand all right," agreed Guard B.

THIRD

INSIDE

I am taught that under *such* circumstances *this* happens. It has been discovered by making the experiment a few times. Not that that would prove anything to us, if it weren't that this experience was surrounded by others which combine with it to form a system. Thus, people did not make experiments just about falling bodies but also about air resistance and all sorts of other things.

But in the end I rely on these experiences, or on the reports of them, I feel no scruples about ordering my own activities in accordance with them.—But hasn't this trust also proved itself? So far as I can judge—yes.

—Ludwig Wittgenstein, *On Certainty*

32

Like many others, at first Menachem loved his father because of who he thought he was, then hated him because of who he actually was, ultimately went back and loved him, this time because of who he tried to be.

No one knew, but in the back of one of the drawers in the big writing desk, the very same desk he hid under as a boy, his father found him there, excited and amazed with his discovery time after time, gathered him up in his arms and flew him around and around in the room, and announced, Rachel look what I found, Rachel look what I found, and Menachem laughed and got excited, and always waited there to be gathered up like that, to be discovered by surprise and gathered up like that, and once his father travelled someplace else, wasn't at home three whole days, and on the morning of the second day Menachem hid there again, under the writing desk, and waited and waited, it seemed to him then like eternity but certainly wasn't more than twenty minutes, and in the end his mother, Rachel, found him there, and spoke to him softly and invited him to eat the eggs that were cold already after more than twenty minutes of waiting on the breakfast table, and she didn't understand why he was so sad and disagreeable, but that was only one time, almost all the other times his dad found him and flew him around and around, but in any case, in the back of one of these drawers in that desk he'd hidden a small box with all the letters he ever received from his father, postcards from abroad and letters from when he was away on reserve service, cards with birthday wishes and other scraps of paper. No one knew. Not even Edna. How did she never find the box? Who knows. In any case she didn't find it.

And this evening he didn't look through it. He sat next to the writing desk and stared into space. When Edna came into the room, he jumped slightly.

Everything okay?

Perfectly okay, said Menachem.

The children are already at the table, she said. You're not coming to eat?

Just a second, honey, said Menachem.

Something bothering you?

No, not at all, answered Menachem. I'm thinking about Motti, you know. What's he doing there, how it is in prison.

Give him a call, suggested Edna, who was a practical woman, even though she was still really shocked by the trial and everything having to do with it. Write a letter. Tell him, I dunno. That he's your friend, that you'll help him get set up when he gets out, that he should hang on and stuff. Things like that.

Forget it, said Menachem. I don't like all that . . . all that . . .

Sentimentality? offered Edna.

Yes, said Menachem. All that sentimentality.

After she left the room he did in fact open the drawer and look at the tattered treasures hidden inside. Sat without moving and looked at them for a long time, as if trying to set them on fire with his eyes. For quite some time no postcard has been added. A longing consumes him.

33

"In short," Guard B says this time to Guard A as they stroll down the corridor with a light step, their bodies free like the land of our fathers, on their way to pass by the door to Motti's cell—actually, from their perspective, on their way to the staff dining hall, but from the perspective of this story the door to Motti's cell is what's important, even though they don't care one bit that this is his cell door, and as they pass by it they don't give it so much as a glance, "in short, this Mahabuta Banana, whatever they called him" (says Guard B, as if he's being dismissive, though actually he's not being dismissive, that's just his way of speaking, these days), "among ourselves we always called him Jimbo and that's all, black as the night he was, maybe his name was Mabruto, go figure, you know what their names are like, anyway we called him Jimbo and that's that, he was lying there under a tree in Grandma's yard may she rest in peace, sleeping like he was dead, worked hard, poor guy, but if you took your eyes off him for a second he disappeared, you have to put those ones on a short leash, the agency told us that too, they said, if we had a Filipino we'd send him over, you can get an honest day's work out of them, the Filipinos, but this one, look, keep a good eye on him and he'll do the work, and he really did the work, all in all, but Grandma, her voice would cut out on her, she could lay in bed for an hour calling him, he would laze around in the yard or something, he once showed me a picture of his wife and kids, cute kids, who knows what's with his wife, no way could I sleep quietly like that with my wife in another country, who knows what she's doing there, and with who, but I'm still not married, don't want to jinx it, may it come quickly, you know, and maybe with them it's fine, a little on the side like that, because here, it's a fact, he would sleep like a baby, and we ourselves were kids then, we didn't think about stuff like that. In short, what was I saying, he was sleeping there under the tree with a Golani beret and one of those end-of-basic-training shirts, I think they make them especially for guys like him, no idea where he got his hands on it. In short, we came to get a cigarette off him, we came quietly, like little elves, and when we pulled out his bundle his passport fell out, and let me tell you, we stuck it in the tree with his hat two meters up, man, what a mess that was, two days he didn't find it, what a mess, we only heard about it later, he turned the whole house upside down, for two whole days he wouldn't leave the house, Grandma went nuts, but in the end he found it" (the voices get weaker and weaker now, at the end of the corridor is another corridor, at its end the dining hall), "told all his friends how the immigration police screwed with him, all over town they took it, in the end they stuck it in the tree, his passport, because they were afraid to hand it over to him, that's what he told everyone, said he told them they'd better watch out for him, he'd fuck them over, to the police he said that. Only we know the truth, but go tell him that now, they made him a national hero, like he threatened the police and all, afterward you couldn't get a day of work out of him. But look, we weren't bad kids. We left him a shekel for the cigarette, like at a kiosk" (according to the laws of physics, sound waves and all that, the voice couldn't carry to Motti's cell throughout this whole story, but in a book it carried well enough, Motti heard every word, the laws are different here, maybe the pages echo or something).

Hours later, at night, Motti lay in his cell, listening to the faint noises or snores and moans and sleeping breaths, and was consumed with regret and flooded with fantasies and so forth, and was nevertheless happy. In his way, he was happy.

34

Edna has a yeast infection.

If I wanted to, I could slice her life into strips of realism.

But not because she's a woman. Because she's a character.

She has a yeast infection, this is quite irritating. And on her right leg the veins form the map of a secret land. She loves her children, and even though their constant demands are sometimes more than she can handle, it turns out they aren't more than she can handle. As evidence: she complies. Even if not always happily. Her brown hair splits at the ends if she doesn't insist on cutting it regularly, therefore she insists on cutting it at least once a month. And once every two to three months she goes to Chaim's salon, who implores her to dye it, and once every two to three months she refuses. Except for that time she assented, and afterward regretted it. Chaim offered to dye everything back, but Edna decided to live with the results. When she was younger and single she was happy to hunker down in the bathroom for a half hour to read a book or magazine. Now she doesn't do this. Over the years her mother's wrinkles have started to crease the sides of her mouth. At first she did silly exercises with her lips, ten or even twenty minutes each day, but it didn't help. She gave up. She once suffered from an ingrown toenail on her right foot (Menachem, too, same thing), and when she brushes her teeth too hard her gums bleed. Her stomach, which was flat, has been curving out nicely since the second pregnancy, but this doesn't bother her. She loves an omelet and bread with cream cheese and olives, like her dad would eat when he got home from work. And once, after their first child, she shaved her genitals entirely, to make them like a little girl's, but Menachem didn't care one way or the other, and so she let the hair grow back. It itched horribly. She was a very serious girl and now she's only a somewhat serious woman. When she was a serious girl she had a cat named Fifi that got lost one day and never came back. Her parents bought her a hamster that ran restlessly in the hopeless wheel in its cage, and after two and a half weeks died from an intestinal virus. She buried him in the garden because she felt that this is what serious girls must do, but she didn't cry. Her parents praised her, what a strong girl, and she hurried inside and locked herself up in her room, so they'd think she was secretly crying there. The truth is she read a book and gnawed on the nails of her left hand. She slept with four men before Menachem. Not all at once. (One of them was actually a teenager. She too was a teenager then. It didn't hurt her. She didn't love him. Or not in retrospect. At the time, when they broke up, she thought she would die. Now she laughs about it, if she thinks about it at all. But laughs with longing. Not for him. For the great drama of adolescence, when everything is so critical. Now it's hard to take anything so seriously.) At the office she puts on a brave face. At home she's a bit tired. Five or six years already she hasn't slept more than five or six hours at night. If they would leave her alone she thinks she could sleep an entire day and wake up fresh as a flower. Actually she would wake up after six hours, maybe six and a half. If she were to survive a plane crash in isolated, ice-capped mountains, she wouldn't be disgusted by cannibalism. One must survive, that much is clear. Should she not survive, she wouldn't kick up a fuss if the others were to eat her flesh. What does she care? She would be dead already. She thinks that the people at work don't know that everything could be otherwise with her, that she easily could go mad or scream, that she could fill her life with wonderful adventures whose nature she doesn't bother to imagine now, but if they were to happen to her, she would enjoy each and every moment. Or she thinks that perhaps the people at work know her very well, actually, and there aren't hidden things like these in her, her life is the only life she could choose. Then she gets a bit sad, then she mocks herself for her pretensions, for her childishness, for these hidden aspirations that aren't appropriate (she thinks) for a woman of her age. But without doubt she could fly to Africa to hunt elephants, only she's not interested in this, and what kind of person wants to kill elephants in the first place. So maybe she couldn't after all. Sometimes she shaves her armpits. Her legs every week. And bleaches her facial hair. And visits her parents once every few days, even without the children. In the evening her back hurts a bit and her legs hurt. In the morning she drinks strong coffee, to shake off sleep and her secret dreams, and only then wakes up the children. And Menachem, of course. Menachem too. She feels obligated to listen to classical music, but nevertheless listens mainly to talk radio. And gets annoyed by the callers to those programs, by what they say and by the vulgar language. Listens nevertheless. And loves cooking with fresh herbs, in moderation. At night with Menachem she prefers to be on top and close her eyes. And when she gets close she opens her eyes and looks right in his face. Sometimes this turns her on. Sometimes turns her off completely. But she can come other ways too. When she's on the bottom. Also from behind. More daring things than this they don't do. Even though each of them thinks about it on their own. Menachem just because, in the middle of the day. And she only when she does it to herself in the shower. She wears makeup in moderation, and prefers her old skirts that have already taken on the shape of her body. And sleeps sometimes in a very, very old shirt that belonged to someone she slept with once. Not the teenager. One of the other ones. How many washings that shirt has gone through since. Not a single cell of his skin remains there. Holes have appeared in it. She loves her clogs too. And the cutting board that she took from her parents' house when she left, it's still with her. She cuts up the most delicious salads on this board. With a new knife. She has a habit of saying what she really means, and then laughing as if this was only a parody of what other people meant, other people entirely, altogether different from her. Her mother does this as well (when she complains to waiters, for example, or wonders why some item or another in some store or another isn't on sale when she would be very interested in buying it if it was). And Edna sometimes recognizes this similarity and is crushed. She doesn't read poetry, though she wrote some once. Gets along with dogs. With cats too. Not with Sweet'N Low. That aftertaste, she thinks, it's something not worth getting used to. And she was proud of herself when she learned to draw out, at work, tables on the computer and to make it so that some of the fields would update themselves, with mathematical functions that sometimes were really complicated. On the back of her hand she has an old scar, impossible to remember what from. She had a root canal once, but has still never taken the car in for an inspection herself. Not because of chauvinism. Out of convenience. Burned-out lights make her sad. She hangs shelves herself. She doesn't play an instrument. Women's magazines annoy her. Once she sprained the small toe on her left foot. Hit it on the doorpost at night, and her eyes filled with tears. Menachem was in the reserves then. She catches colds easily. A pack of tissues is hidden in a drawer at work. She doesn't need glasses. Or maybe just for reading. Her shoulders are just the right width. When she breastfed, her nipples cracked. When she was a teenager, the signs of her growing sexuality made her rebellious. More than this: they outright offended her. That all at once the world reduced her to the status of a biological machine—this is the organ for mating and this is for breast feeding, and the widening hips are for giving birth one day, and the blood that synchronizes all this comes once a month (regular as a clock, with her). Now, go figure why, she finds beauty in all that. Comfort even. At the time she thought that her sexual organ was like a wound gaping out at the world. Sometimes she still thinks this. Her breasts have become like the anchor that attaches her to the (relatively) stable ground of life. She won't tolerate dirty fingernails. Nor insects. She doesn't like hearing her own recorded voice. Quickly erases messages that she left on the answering machine at home. They really disgust her. Never smoked much. Only in social situations. And sometimes, as I pointed out, she's had it up to here (she indicates with her hand at the height of her forehead, even higher than that). And she shouldn't strain her left hand. It starts to hurt very quickly. In the years to come it will get worse, the pain will take much longer to pass. That's how the body is. Once she got burned by an extremely hot frying pan. She's burned her tongue many times. She eats quickly, but enjoys it. Work's fine for her. She believes she can hold on until retirement. When she complains about a stomachache, for instance, and Menachem laughs and says, get out of here, you'll bury all of us in the end, she gets angry and says, how can you talk like that? What kind of a terrible thing is that to say to a mother? But usually she isn't dramatic like that, and when her cheek itches, she scratches it absentmindedly. Sometimes she eats falafel while standing. Sometimes she just finishes the kids' portions. When she was small and her mother would cover her face with both hands in play, she would be terrified. Who knows what kind of face would be there when she removed her hands. After this too some time would pass until she calmed down. Who knows what kind of face was there before she removed them. But now she's no longer a girl, and in her tummy delicate cells are multiplying. I give the baby eighty-three years at the most. Eighty-seven, on average, if it's a girl. Eighty-two if an Arab citizen of Israel (though the chances are slim). It will be a boy, in fact, and he will be the one she loves the most, though she won't admit this to anyone ever, and after two or three years she'll be pregnant again and he'll say to her, Mom, I want always to be your littlest, littlest boy, and within a week she'll have an abortion, won't say a word about it to anyone, years later she'll tell him, not in order to demand anything or hurt him, she'll just tell him, as a fact, so he'll know how much she loves him, how much she always loved him, from the beginning. And this abortion won't result in an infection and there will be no gynecological damage and no feelings of guilt, she won't have to pay any price of that sort. All it will do is shake up the living boy when she finally tells him, he'll already be grown up then, he'll go and tell his spouse, she'll think that it's totally screwed up, but all that is no longer our concern.

35

They'll clink glasses full of Diet Coke for the New Year. "This is
for a sweet year," she'll say, "by whatever means necessary," and
they'll laugh. Every year they'll do this. They'll have lots of little
jokes like this. They'll be one of those couples who make other
couples jealous, old now, sitting, say, on a bench on a street next
to a governmental office and holding hands or him stroking her
hair absentmindedly, for fifty years now he's been stroking her hair
absentmindedly, and they know one another inside and out, and
after all these years they are still so beautiful in each other's eyes.
And Ariella, she . . .

This line of thought, this strand of thought, Guard B cuts off.
"You holding up in here, man?" he asks Motti chummily through
the barred hatch on the door. We didn't expect this chumminess.
After all: a guard. "It takes some getting used to here, I know," B
smiles at him. "If there's a problem, if you need something, just say
the word. We're also here to help," and Motti responds, and means
it, "Everything's fine, uh, man."

And when he says this, at the same actual moment, Menachem
turns over in bed and turns his back on Edna, so she won't see his
eyes that are suddenly red, so she won't hear his heart go wild on

him because he thought about Motti, because he thought about his great debt, because he thought who knows what's happening to Motti now, what's with him there, maybe they're raping him in the ass, stealing cigarettes from him, you know, the kind of things they do in the big house. But Motti is okay. Just fine. And he's quieter than he was until now. It's hot in the cell, so hot there, and the food isn't the kind you get used to, but in his head he takes off and goes, one two and he's already on his way, a space of infinite possibilities opens up to him like a giant sail and he sails to wherever he wants. Whereas Menachem doesn't sail anyplace, just gets out of bed slowly and goes down the hallway, and sits down next to Laika who's breathing deeply in sleep, lying there like her bones were magnetized to the floor, and he pets her—she wakes up and turns her head, then goes back to dozing, disinterested—and he sits next to her for hours on end, he thinks, even though actually only four or five minutes have passed, and then he goes to the bathroom, washes his face, urinates, looks in the mirror, returns to bed, turns over and over, thinks about Motti, what's with him, what's happening to him there, must suffer terribly, oh, the debt, this heavy debt, a chain that binds him to the world and there's no escape, he feels it on his ankles, it fills his lungs until the air is pushed out, this a debt that can't be paid off, enslavement worse than the mortgage, even, he's almost angry now, how can you be expected to fall asleep like this, when's Yom Kippur coming, maybe he'll fast this year, he turns over and over, eventually falls asleep, in his sleep completely normal dreams visit him, whereas Edna, who's physically very close to him, the blanket over them like a protective tent, in her dream she's entirely abandoned in space. Again the same dream:

just her in a spacesuit, her spaceship gets farther and farther away, only the glass of the helmet separates Edna from the nothingness. This dream comes to her from that movie they saw together, a man is tossed out among the stars, carried far away from the ship, cord cut, damn Menachem for taking her to such a fucked-up movie in the first place, for years now it hasn't left her head, in her dream she's thrown into a black nothingness. And it's not the suffocating that's scariest, but rather this drifting, completely alone, in the emptiness and the cold, you can kick and shriek and lash out with your hands, it's all pointless, soon your air will run out, a few hours all told, and despite this maybe it's better to just remove your helmet and wait for your lungs to explode from the difference in pressure (in order to not break the cosmic law of the equilibrium of pressure the dreaming Edna will explode from the inside like a hot dog cooked too long; the little bit of air in her lungs will transform into ice crystals and float far away). There isn't anything anywhere, and the meaning of the dream outside the world of dream may be the reason for her sticking with Menachem and all that. It's easier, they say, not to drift off alone until death, and it's not just a matter of comforting or distracting yourself; it's also sticking a foot in the door to the future we won't see, here are our faces renewed in the faces of our children. But where does all this get us, where does it get us if Edna is still drifting through the nothingness but now hand in hand with her small family, how fragile everything is, all the time looking each other in the face, waiting to see who would be hurled into space without a suit and who will explode first, she or Menachem, maybe the children, God forbid. But she doesn't remember them. I don't mean the children. She remembers them well enough.

I mean the terrible dreams. She won't remember when she wakes up. Lucky.

"You know," continues the Guard, who already went away down the corridor after a moment of uncomfortable silence and then returned, leaned against the wall next to Motti's door and played around with the toes of his feet in his shoe, maybe his athlete's foot is starting up again there, "I didn't really know my father."

"Really?" asks Motti, this thickheaded candor surprising him, and justly.

"Swear on my mother," the Guard says seriously. "He would drink like a fish. You wouldn't see him for two years, suddenly he would show up in my room to cry and curse. His whole life he never learned to read. Poor guy."

"Poor guy," agreed Motti.

"Yes," the Guard agreed too. "He kidnapped me, took me to the forest once. Damned if I know where he found a forest here, but he kidnapped me and took me there. In the end, I escaped."

"Sounds complicated," said Motti, because you have to say something.

"Complicated," confirmed the Guard. "He was a miserable person. I feared for my life around him. Do you know they built an island in the middle of the Yarkon River? There's a whole story about it, I'll tell you some time."

"I'd be happy to hear," said Motti politely, though islands didn't interest him much.

"So I'll tell you some time," repeated the Guard. "There were some real scenes."

"Great," said Motti.

"Yeah. Okay, I've got to go now, okay? Tell me if you need something."

"I will," promised Motti.

"You look like a good guy to me," said the Guard. "Too bad you wound up here."

"Too bad," agreed Motti.

"So good night, right?"

"Good night," said Motti.

"Drunk driving, huh," said Guard B.

"Yes," said Motti.

"My father would drink a lot too," said Guard B. "I said that already."

"You did," said Motti.

The Guard walked off, then returned, was quiet, walked off again.

Motti waited another moment. So, an island in the middle of the Yarkon. Then he wandered around and around in his narrow cell like a puppy looking for a place for himself, even though in the end he didn't curl up sleepily but rather sat down on the stool, sat down and curled up there, cheek to the cold wall, and in spite of everything a sort of moan escaped from his mouth and his body slackened. Sat there and relaxed. A wall is a wall, what is there to say. Were he to close his eyes, he could imagine that Ariella is still on the other side.

36

And we're so cautious. So cautious even in love, especially in love, fearful of losing control, ashamed that we're not losing control. But if we lose it, everything will collapse. Our boundaries, our beautiful boundaries, the wonderful limitations that make us the people we are, that give form to our books, to our good books, to our bad books, to our families, to our wolf packs, with the people and the dogs and the other beings inside them, with our TV news and the articles in our newspapers, with our paintings and the musical works we send off like interstellar dispatches, full of hidden ideas, with performances, even, with the strange ideas we hold on to, afraid to let go, with our odd logic, with the things that seem acceptable to us, for instance transporting people from continent to continent in order to work for us for next to nothing and afterward sending them back again, and other things as well, for instance going out each and every morning to feed cats in the street, to pet iguanas, dropping proclamations from light aircraft, diving, parachuting, striving, changing, regretting, watching reality television.

And if it was up to me, I would write fragile books that from their first pages would be like those Chinese vases, thin as eggshell, so thin they're almost just the idea of a border, marking out the world that they contain and marked by it as well, from within and without. So it's possible to break them into a hundred little pieces and glue them together again crooked, and that's what I would do, glue them with children's paste, use masking tape even. It's possible to work on this gluing hour after hour, work on this unsightly reconstruction, full of love. In the end it would be possible to use them for something, these deformed things. To put a flower inside, to caress them (these vases, the books) without fear. See, they were already broken.

37

Listen, my brother, said Menachem, you know they don't allow people to bring beer in here? A full six pack I brought you, the whore at the entrance is drinking them right now for sure.

Nonsense, said Motti.

So what, asked Menachem, how are you holding up?

Holding up, said Motti. No big deal.

They're treating you okay, wondered Menachem.

Just fine, answered Motti. They were quiet for a moment.

Is Laika okay? Asked Motti.

Just fine. The kids are crazy about her, answered Menachem. So you're holding up, yeah?

Holding up, repeated Motti.

We need to come up with a plan for you, declared Menachem.

A plan?

A plan. What you'll do when you get out of here. What you'll do with your life, what you'll achieve. Goals, Menachem pointed out. Prioritize goals. Be proactive. Decide what you want and go for it, you hear? Here, he said. Look at me.

So, said Motti.

So what, asked Menachem.

I'm looking at you, said Motti.

Hah! laughed Menachem. You bastard, what a bastard. I'm crazy about you. Maybe, he continued, maybe you'll come work with me. I'll fix you up with something, it's a great start, I'm telling you. Did you lease your place?

No, answered Motti. Someone in my place, digging through my things . . . that's not . . . I don't want that.

Definitely not, agreed Menachem.

And it's not that I have bills to pay, added Motti.

Definitely not, confirmed Menachem.

Other than property tax, corrected Motti.

Other than property tax, agreed Menachem again, thought for a moment and then said, I'll cover that for you, man.

Thanks, said Motti.

Nothing to it, said Menachem and peeked at his watch. Nothing to it. So what, he strained to laugh, did you see the ass on that guard? I'd give it to her in a second.

Um, said Motti.

When you get out of here, promised Menachem, I'll get a thousand whores for you. At the same time, yeah?

No need, said Motti and looked at the table. Just take care of Laika, okay?

No question, said Menachem. And the property tax as well, yeah?

And the property tax, agreed Motti.

Good, said Menachem and looked again at his watch intently. I've got to go, Edna's birthday today.

Of course, of course, said Motti. I didn't know it was today. Send her congratulations from me, yeah? You didn't have to come today if it's her birthday and stuff.

Nonsense, said Menachem and got up. Today's Wednesday, no?

Wednesday, confirmed Motti.

So we'll see each other next week, yeah, man?

Of course, of course, said Motti.

Or maybe not next week, said Menachem suddenly. I was thinking about taking Edna abroad for a bit. A few days, you know. She deserves it.

Deserves it, said Motti. Definitely deserves it.

But the Wednesday after that I'm here, yeah?

I'm not going anywhere, said Motti.

Of course, of course, Menachem said now. You know that I owe you, yeah?

Nonsense, said Motti. You're like a brother to me. You are, you know.

38

And after Menachem left, Motti thought, I should have prepared him a list for Laika. Write down the things she loves to do, so she won't be miserable. (And in the back of his mind a voice also said, no, I shouldn't have prepared him a list. So she won't love him like she does me. So she'll want to come back to me when I get out. He quickly silenced it, this voice.)

Because he, Motti, is her owner. Even the municipal documents say so, in writing. Therefore it's necessary to tell Menachem if she likes raw sausages or leftover steak, if she likes when you throw her a ball, so she'll fetch it, or if she doesn't understand why you've taken it from her and thrown it, the small ball that she gnaws so diligently. Did he tell Menachem not to let her out on the street without a leash? Certainly he told him. No need for a muzzle, for sure he told him that too, even though now he doesn't remember.

"In short," Guard B said after he returned to Motti's cell and sat down, folding his legs and hoping for a glass of cold, freezing, water, except that kind of thing can't be found in prison, and he looked at the vague and stupid marks drawn on the plaster, "In short," he said again, even though there was nothing short about it, "Jimbo sits there, see, with those pictures, and cries like a little boy. Look, he says to me, even though I'm already looking. Look at that sweet girl, how did I leave her? Oh, oh, my girl, he says. I promise you I'll return soon. And how many pictures he had! Well, not many, actually. Maybe five. And that's my wife, he tells me for maybe the thousandth time. Pretty, no? Prettiest in the neighborhood. Or prettiest in the village or wherever he came from. Oh, oh, my wife, he says. He had a tendency to repeat himself, you understand. Oh, oh. Lucky that there are cameras, no? Think how it would be if we all just had to remember. In the end we wouldn't recognize anyone. Here," he says, "look at me. Every time I imagine my family, I see someone else. That's how it is. So many years have passed."

"So many," repeated Motti unintentionally.

"Lots," confirmed Guard B, "Lots and lots. No one left. Just me. Alone. Alone like a dog is alone. Dad I already told you about, Mom, you know. I had a little sister, but she's gone too. Choked on a chicken bone. Got stuck in her foodpipe. And that was the end of her. Comma."

"Oh, she went into a coma?" asked Motti.

"No," said the guard. "Died right there, on the spot."

"So that was the end of her, period, you mean," Motti said.

"No, no," countered Guard B. "Hadn't gotten her period yet. She was so young. Wasn't ten years old when she went."

39

They acclimated her, Laika (that is, the historical Laika, the actual one, and prior to this her name was Kudryavka and she flew into space and died) to eat gelatinized food. Jelly. Because that's the food she would get in the spaceship. They kept her, Moshka, and Albina in smaller and smaller cages, so they'd get acclimated to that too, and put them in flight simulators, so they'd get acclimated to the pressure of liftoff. Albina, before her, went up twice on a missile. Moshka was used in order to check the systems in the cabin, life support and the like.

The Russians, as the BBC website reported a few years ago, said she died after a week. As previously stated before, it wasn't like that at all. (Barely a few hours. Maybe better that way. Suffered less.) The spaceship she flew in weighed 508 kilograms. She herself weighed approximately six. Only after liftoff did they say she wouldn't return and wasn't meant to from the beginning. She was fastened in so that she wouldn't just tumble around inside the cabin, which was pretty small in any case. The spaceship returned on April 14, 1958, around five months after it was launched, and it burned up in the atmosphere upon reentry (and if someone made a wish then, thinking it was a shooting star, it's quite possible this person is still alive—you could find him and ask what he wished for and if it materialized in the end).

I imagined the Laika in this book as a German shepherd, but everyone else can imagine her however they like. The dead Laika was, they say, of extremely mixed parentage. The beating of her heart accelerated threefold after liftoff. They had already put her in the cabin three days before ignition. Georgi Grechko, who was a cosmonaut, said that the spaceship, the satellite that Laika was sent up in, didn't separate properly from the missile with which it launched. Perhaps the systems were damaged, and therefore Laika was baked inside her skin. Forty years after this, her likeness was engraved on the monument to fallen cosmonauts, near Moscow. I doubt this did her any good.

Look at her picture on the cover. A paw resting almost playfully, an ear bent mischievously, I think, or maybe because genetics made it so. It appears that she's smiling, definitely smiling, I don't see fear in that look, but who am I to recognize her fear.

4□

"You listening?" Guard B made sure. "I'm standing there with that hat in front of Tom's aunt. Middle of the heat wave, I'm telling you, and I feel the butter I put there start to drip. And she's talking, the aunt, she goes on and on—and I'm feeling how it's already starting to drip, you know? Onto my forehead and the neck and all that. And she stops speaking suddenly, starts staring at me, I thought I was going to die on the spot. Jumps on me and takes off the hat, I thought I was dead, suddenly she hugs me. God Almighty! she says. I thought the boy's brain was starting to leak out on him here. Why are you walking around with butter inside your hat, you strange boy?"

"Funny," said Motti.

"Funny?" Guard B was amazed. "I almost frightened her to death. What's funny about that? You don't know how awful that was for me. What, like I don't know what it is to worry that some-one's going to die right in front of your eyes? Just like that, with my own eyes, I saw my mother die."

"I'm sorry," said Motti.

"It's not your fault," said Guard B, "and it also happened a long time back."

"What did she die from?" asked Motti.

"From the disease," said Guard B.

"What disease?" asked Motti.

"The disease, the disease," said Guard B impatiently and meant cancer, which many people don't call by its name out of fear that it's an actual, proper name, like the kind you call someone with, so it (the cancer) might come. Just like you don't speak the Name itself, you know the one, as though there's a big eye in the heavens that will open up as soon as you call by name that which cannot be mentioned. (I too never speak that Name aloud. I never say, *Yahweh*—but look, I wrote it, that much I did. Which, actually, is a little defensive strategy I've put together for my book. Now, in certain circles, it will have to go straight to the *geniza*, thank God, to be stored indefinitely.) "Right in front of my eyes, she died on me."

"I'm sorry," said Motti again, because what else can you say. "That's tough, to see your mom like that for the last time."

"If only, if only that was the last time," said Guard B and lowered his voice. "In my dreams she still comes to me, that one. A few years dead already, and still coming. I've made myself sick over it," he said. "Her and her underhanded death games. But, in any case," he said philosophically, then cleared his throat. "Where was I?"

"With the butter," said Motti.

"Yes, the butter. The whole hat was completely ruined. Did I already tell you what we would need that butter for?"

"No," said Motti. "You didn't say."

"C'mon," said Guard B. "What kind of shitty person am I, anyway. Don't know how to tell a lousy story. Did I already tell you about how Jimbo went to jail?"

"No," said Motti.

"Well, look," said Guard B. "How can I expect you to understand anything? And what about the house that floats on the Yarkon? Did I say anything about that?"

"Not a thing," said Motti.

"Well, well, well," concluded Guard B. "You see? This is exactly what I'm talking about."

41

Maybe (thought Motti a few hours, maybe days, after this; no one was standing outside his cell now, certainly not Guard B), maybe she ran away and got run over and now she's lying on the side of the road, her leg broken and bleeding, and she's whimpering in pain. She doesn't know why this happened to her, why this pain. She doesn't even wonder about it, doesn't resent it, isn't mad, isn't saying she doesn't deserve any of this, doesn't deserve this suffering, she's such a good dog. Motti, in his cell, cries bitterly. For the first time in this book he sits there and cries bitterly.

Only nothing's happened. Not yet. Motti is in his cell and Laika is in the hallway of Menachem and Edna's house, sleeping.

And then he passed by there, down one of the jail's corridors, Guard B. He's already finished his shift and is on his way outside and then home, grateful that he doesn't have to stay here like all the unfortunate inmates, though also feeling a bit unpleasant because of this.

He's a big man, and so easily embarrassed, his name should have been Irving, or Percival. But no, it wasn't meant to be.

And more than once, by the way, whenever Guard B went back early, during the day, to his dark house—if he forgot his car keys, for example, if he left his cell phone on the dining room table—would it seem to him that he felt the vestiges of some presence in the house, the tail end of the air that someone else might have breathed, a shadow slipping away along a wall just before he could see it, not even caught in the corner of his eye. And yet, he's still convinced that one day, if for instance he forgets his driver's license next to the telephone, then goes back home where everything is dark, he'll clearly feel, without a doubt, that someone, someone is there, that many are there, and then he'll close the door and won't leave, he'll close it behind him and remain inside, the door to his back and he in the dark, and they'll come out. In the meantime he hasn't had the courage to try. Because he worries they'll appear suddenly and because he's embarrassed by his belief that they'll appear.

In some senses he's like one of those rodents—the shy ones. Every touch startles him, and sometimes he looks at himself from the outside, as it were, and reprimands himself. You idiot, he says to himself, for example. What's your problem, you idiot? But he isn't an idiot, and this isn't his problem. His problem is that he's lived to be over fifty, thank God, and despite this he's still known to turn around when someone in the street behind him calls out, "Hey, kid!"

Tonight, in any case, Guard B (whose name is neither Irving nor Percival) passes by Motti's cell and this sobbing comes from inside, this heartrending sobbing.

He too would cry if they left him like this, alone in a cell. Therefore he stops by the door and waits a moment, to see if the sound subsides. And when it doesn't subside he knocks softly.

"Everything okay with you, man?" He asks. "You need something?"

"It's my dog," Motti says, "I think something terrible happened to her."

"Is she there in the cell?" Guard B is alarmed, since it is absolutely and strictly forbidden to bring animals inside the prison.

"No, no," says Motti, "She's at the house of my friend Menachem."

"I'm sure she's fine," says Guard B, hesitantly. Motti doesn't answer.

"Do you want to call him," offers Guard B in a whisper. He's forbidden to offer things like that, he could get fired. "I'll bring you my cell phone, don't tell anyone."

"That would be great," says Motti and wipes his nose.

"Here, here," Guard B extends his phone through the hatch. "Call quick."

And Motti calls. Two in the morning now, but he calls.

Menachem answers, panic-stricken. Hello? Who is this? He asks. Motti? What happened?

Is Laika okay? Motti asks quickly.

She's here at home sleeping. Do you what time it is, you psycho? It's two in the morning now. You woke the kids.

I'm sorry, Menachem, Motti says. Tell Edna that I'm sorry too. I had a horrible feeling, you know.

C'mon, it's okay, says Menachem. But try saving your awful feelings for normal hours, okay? You woke the kids.

I'm sorry, Menachem, Motti says again. Pet her on the tummy for me.

Sure, sure, and Menachem hangs up. And to Edna, who woke up panic-stricken as well—parents often wake up panic-stricken—to Edna he says, that motherfucker Motti sure picked some time to call.

He always was a bit strange, says Edna, nearly asleep.

Motherfucker, Menachem says again before he falls asleep.

Nothing can happen to her, to Laika. In the beautiful stories he tells himself she's often there, with him and with Ariella. Walking in fields, sitting on benches, watching television, stuff like that.

42

And what's with Laika, really? This very much disturbs me, that she has no personality. Half a book already written and she has no personality. Half a book—and I've only just noticed it. What an embarrassment this is, especially for a book that preaches so much—and with such immense self-righteousness.

In short, what's with Laika? What kind of dog is she? Lively and playful and full of energy? Affectionate? Does she love people? Does she sleep a lot? Did she ever chew up Motti's library? Chew up his shoes? And how long did it take her to learn not to relieve herself in the house?

Her history doesn't interest me here. It doesn't matter if she came to Motti as a puppy or already full grown. It only matters what she's like, what gives her pleasure, what makes her suffer. Like the rest of the characters here, all the details of her past are just cheap gossip as far as I'm concerned.

And so: Laika is a good dog. She doesn't have hip or skin problems, she has good teeth, a not-too-sensitive digestive system, good instincts, sharp hearing, a refined sense of smell. She doesn't bark excessively at night, wags her tail when you get home. Chases cats, but doesn't catch them. And not because she can't catch them, but rather because she's not interested in this. It's a game for her, not hunting. Loves it when you pet her on the tummy and scratch her behind her ears, a thing Edna does wonderfully; for hours they can sit like that together, Edna watching television or paging through a magazine, her free hand scratching Laika behind the ear. Such pleasure this is! Whoever isn't a dog just can't understand, not even if you love it when someone pets you on the tummy, not even if you wiggle your hind leg when they pet you there.

What else can be said about a dog's personality? As with people, there's no real point talking about it. Either you know them or you don't, why go into detail? Maybe just to fill up some extra pages so your book won't be too short (a novella), but instead will weigh what it needs to, so people will feel like they're getting their money's worth.

Laika, in any case, loves things that move. Drag a towel or a toy in front of her—she'll jump at it immediately, grab it with her teeth and pull. What's the difference between these toys and those living cats: these that she catches and those that she doesn't? What's the difference from her perspective, that is? How does she tell them apart? Hour after hour, by the way, she can lie hypnotized and watch the hamster running on his small wheel in the children's room.

Their lives (when Motti feels better) will be like reality TV or like the life of a religious person: an eye on them at all times (it will be her, looking at him at all times), and thus they'll strive at all times to be worthy, to live for real. They won't waste time on nonsense like me ("the narrator") and Motti do here. We are indeed in the same exact situation. We could have done something good with our lives. We could have been helpful to someone. We could have loved, been loved, really helped, like he and Laika could as well. Save a life. Many lives. Save as many lives as possible. Walk around in the streets saving kittens. Volunteering at animal shelters. This would certainly raise one's spirits. And in order to make Ariella happy he'll take care of his body. He'll go, let's say, to a gym. And she'll laugh at him, look, look how you've puffed up, what a man I have, what a man, she'll laugh, but she'll actually love those new muscles, they will touch her deep down inside, on an evolutionary level, she'll be drawn to him, she'll want to touch him all the time, to feel those new muscles, well-defined no less. At the shelter he'll toss around bags of food. Lift up enormous dogs onto the operating table. Build walls, straighten fences. He'll gently pet puppies with his massive hands, so they'll get used to being touched by humans. And when someone shows up there to abandon, for example, a grown dog who's been with this someone for years (no lack of excuses, never a lack, and I've already heard about one, ten years old, whose owner abandoned her because she was no longer able to reproduce, he was used to selling her offspring for money; and I've already heard the one that goes our children are no longer attached to him, he's already grown, we were thinking about getting a new puppy instead; about how it's getting cold at night now, inconvenient to have to take him out on a walk; and then how, after three years together, three or four or even eight, we just had to take the dog back, they say, no longer a good fit, but look how cute he is, someone will definitely take him, give us a call, tell us how he's doing, give us an update, after all we love him a lot, bye bye . . . and it could very well be that you too are one of those people who throw your dogs away willy-nilly, and don't see what the problem is at all: toss them out of the car, let's say, on the way to the airport to head out of town—stop on the way to Ben Gurion Airport, open the car door, and shove the dog out, good-bye; and, look, if that's the case, a miserable and gruesome death is far too lenient of a punishment for you, and unnecessary, actually, because if you have children, and of course you do, when they get older they'll abandon you to rot in some stinking old-folks home, to rot in your filthy diapers: they'll come to visit once a week or every other week for a half hour, reluctantly, and will talk about nonsense with a forced smile, and this will be a quite fitting end, good luck to you and I hope you burn), when this man shows up there to abandon his dog, Motti will spit in his face. Will stand opposite him, with his new muscles, and will spit. Will say to him, listen, the usual practice here is to request a small donation from people bringing dogs to the shelter, but I'll gladly donate even a thousand shekels in your name if in exchange you'll just allow me to give you something you need. And when the man says, yes, yes (here it comes), Motti will spit in his face. Then he'll turn his big body around, his shirt too small to contain this firm abundance, and he'll walk away laughing, even run off mischievously, giggling hee hee.

Only he won't really have the courage or lack of manners to do this. Not his fault. And I don't have the courage to cause him to do this. To intentionally take an action from which, by definition, there is no return. A thing that would actually exist in the world, that would leave evidence behind in the form of the spit dripping down the man's face, lips, the curve of his chin.

I, by contrast, if I could do it, wouldn't bother to spit. I would loosen the man's jaw. With one punch. And so too for the man who abused my Cookie, even though that's not what they called her, my dog, back then—who knows if she had a name at all. Nevertheless, they kicked her. Every time she stood up, they kicked her, and when we first met she would lie down helplessly and break out shrieking if someone so much as put a hand on her, just put it out to pet her. One devastating punch for the man who, we're guessing, stepped on her snout, since her jaw never healed properly. Who did this, who? What's more, I know her now, and can see in my mind's eye how she got up after the first kick, maybe even the second, still wanting to be petted. Yearning for a touch and fearing it too, like she does now, and as she would after the kick, lying on her back and howling with longing, with fear, hoping to be petted this time, not the other thing. No, not one punch. Many more than one. To cause pain as he caused pain, including a foot to the jaw. Even though, of course, he didn't do it out of absolute evil, there is no absolute evil, he kicked, of course, out of misery. But that doesn't absolve him. And the punch, well, but no, this too is a lie. I wouldn't do a thing. Afterward I would regret it, regret not doing it, that much is clear, but I wouldn't do a thing. I'm just trying to push this novel, this narrator's voice, past its limits. So it will explode, so it will burst. One can drown in this expanse of possibilities, die from too much revulsion and joy, die from this desire to abstain, from the desire for nothing to happen, for everything to remain open. I've already said this, I know, said it one too many times. But Sarah's dead and this didn't really accomplish a thing. Her life reached its limit— only Motti, even in his prison cell, is still drenched in possibilities like rain. And the more I limit him—if he's sent to solitary confinement, even—his freedom to avoid choosing only grows stronger. The freedom, that is, to narrate, to fabricate, to take pleasure in the things that could be.

It certainly would have been better if these issues hadn't come up in this monologue of mine. If they had come up in a dialogue between two characters, with complicated psychological motivations. But they're true either way.

Whereas Sarah died, as mentioned, and this had almost no influence. Everything is so clean here, clean and well ordered, and there's no way out. Where's the bathroom in the prison, where does Motti shower, what kind of smell lingers there, and who are the other inmates, do they use deodorant and where do they brush their teeth, and where is the world, where is it with all its beloved, insufferable disparities. Where is it imprisoned for us, it is we who imprison it, closing ourselves up in our perfect rooms, in the knowing, barren cell of our story, of our perfect fantasy about ourselves, about our beloveds who we meet with less and less, having complete conversations in our heads, but with our bodies, no, nothing doing. There's nothing in here, is there, from out in the world, nothing makes it inside, not the smell, the temperature, the soil, the plastic, the air, the worms, the ads, the demonstrations and counterdemonstrations, the full plates, the sinks of dirty dishes afterward, the rain, the humidity, the actual memory of things that actually were—if there's any such thing, I mean distinct somehow from the memory of things that never were. So I now want to condemn it, this novel. Condemn it entirely, breach its clean borders, the imperative of its borders. I don't want to go on playing the voice of wisdom, as it were, being the one who knows. So perhaps it would be better to try again, no? It would be better to start over. This time on a smaller scale. To start with a shriek interrupted and with the noise of the metal grating in the fallen cage, with blood and shreds of fur, with Edna who hurries to throw up in the bathroom: because something happened here, there's no denying it. Something that's impossible to undo, impossible to pretend that it never was, even though that's exactly what Edna (like me) tries to do.

And she reprimands Laika. Bad dog! she tells her. What did you do? What did you do, bad dog? And points at the shreds, at the mangled fur. Only Laika just looks at the pointing finger. She doesn't understand. And why would she understand. And even after Edna's already cleaned everything, even then she doesn't look at Laika, doesn't pet her, though she knows intellectually that there was no malicious intent here, no guilt, it was just an act and that's all, she doesn't succeed in bringing herself to look at that fucking dog. She hurries to the store before the children come home and buys a new hamster. No one will notice that anything is different, other than that the cage has been placed on the table, up high and far from Laika. Yuck, murderer.

Is this the moral? Edna doesn't ask this herself, but we definitely do. Is this the moral? Is there no encounter that doesn't end with teeth? With tearing?

44

Well, something happened. Something happened that's impossible to ignore. There was the gathering up and there was the rinsing in water, there were the bleach and the rag that was also thrown into the garbage, to cover up the remains, and even before all this there had been the hamster's rapid heartbeats, his instantaneous, absolute terror, the pain when those teeth were sunk into him, his cry, the additional pain when what was torn was torn, his last heartbeat, the absence of pain, the darkness if there was darkness. And already a new hamster in the cage, far above on the table, no one will know that anything happened here, Edna won't say a thing, why upset the children—but all these things were, definitely were, but where are they now, what are the ramifications for the plot, this is not known.

And if I had the talent for it, I wouldn't make a story out of all this, but a dollhouse instead. Look: this is Sarah's empty room, who dressed warm, ate something small, drank a cup of coffee with Sweet'N Low, then left the house and that's all. And here, in a different room, a metal doll in the shape of Edna lies in bed, and she dreams a bad dream. It doesn't seep into Menachem's sleep, who lies beside her, since dreams don't seep anywhere. She dreams, for example, about her son who has yet to be born, he stands in the middle of a field of smoke, behind him are trampling war machines and chunks of earth rise up in the air because of the bombing, and Edna looks at him with an indescribable sadness as he calls to her as if nothing happened even though his shirt is soaked in blood and tissue, completely torn up in the places where once he had arms and now there are only shreds of flesh that he raises as he calls to her laughingly, "Look, Ma! No hands!" This a very common dream in this country.

In another room, out of scraps of dark paper: sky-darkening trees, a ground carpeted in needles hiding sharp rocks, perhaps later a moon lacking color rising above, and amid all this the river from Guard B's stories flows along in fog, and in the background his friend Tom stands, whose parents had a store in State Square, he was probably the first child in Israel with this name. And he had a brother named Lace and another brother named Crane and a sister, Thrion they called her, and all of them very much loved exciting adventure stories.

Another room will be the prison cell. And another one, on the other side of a thin partition, made perhaps out of popsicle sticks, will be the empty abode of Motti in his home. High, high above, far off in the sky, a plane will pass by. There will be another room there, another whole wing, a giant library containing Motti's marvelous future. In the meantime, he isn't too involved with the world, tries hard to avoid it, but in the future he'll get involved—now he isn't a father, but he'll even be a father then. Establish rules, attend to things. And not arbitrarily. Not the way we punish a kid and say to him, and so to ourselves as well, this is a learning experience, when actually we mean: this is what our own father did to us, in his day—and we still don't really get the point.

A doghouse will be there too, in this dollhouse. It too is empty, since Laika was never forced to live in a doghouse. Her whole life she will sleep next to beds and even on them, and people will pet her at night.

But it's also possible to make a different shape in space, in place of this story. To make out of papier-mâché or even clockwork various tracks that people could hurry down, like those cardboard decoys dogs chase at the races, but, in this case, each one magnetized to the others (I mean, the rushing cardboard people). And in fact it's lucky that the speed of the cardboard people is greater than the force of attraction, so that each one still stays on its track. Otherwise, they would crash into each other with all the terrible force of their acceleration, and nothing would remain of them.

45

Motti saw, on his small stool, really saw, with his own eyes, how he and the chubby Ariella (because of her pregnancy) would stroll and hold hands in the street, and then, even better than this, don't hold hands directly, but rather each one of them holds a hand of the small girl who walks between them, and every three steps they lift her in the air, hup, hup, and by now she's choking from all the excitement of this familiar occurrence, every three steps—look, two more, one more, and now—being lifted up into the air and then returning to the ground and so on again and again. Galit, they'll call her. The girl. The three of them will walk in the street and Ariella with her tummy. A lollipop, too, he would put there, in this picture, if it weren't for the fact that Galit's two hands are busy with their hands, so they can lift her. Maybe the lollipop will be in her mouth, if so. The three of them will go to a puppet show, let's say. And he and Ariella will be just amazed at her trust, amazed at Galit's uncompromising acceptance of everything that happens on the tiny stage. It will astound them how the children sit there truly hypnotized, they don't pick up on a single one of the production's contradictions, giving themselves like this to the pleasure, none of them being the least bit restless, whereas he, Motti, it seems to him that he always was a problematic boy, even as a boy he was a problem, never once really enjoyed himself, always stealing a glance to the side to see how people expected him to have fun, and then tried to look as though he was, but no, not now, there's no place here for this self-pity, for this futile, idiotic longing. This isn't his second chance. This is her first chance, what's her name, Galit. And how much fun she's having! On the stage is a mouse, a mouse puppet, with a knight's sword and a crown. And the children, as one person, laugh in the right places, hold their breath in the right places, breathe again right after. And then the three of them will leave, at the end of the performance. After they applaud until their fingers almost hurt, such a wonderful play it was, they'll come again to see it next chance they get, and at home they'll cut up a cardboard box, make a window in it, and Ariella will sew small curtains, and in the evening, instead of television, they'll put on small performances for each other. The heart breaks, it does.

On his little stool he sees all this. All these worlds open up to him. And then the voice of Guard B invades. His nasal, annoying voice. "And then we set sail!" he says. "Would you believe it? Me and Jimbo sail down the Yarkon River inside a small boat. The immigration police on his trail—but we're in the boat. Like it's the Mississippi, I swear."

"Uh huh," says Motti politely but grudgingly. Galit dissolves, as does Ariella.

"And we're there," continues the guard. "Rowing like crazy in that little boat, I swear, I think about it now and see us like in a movie, makes me laugh, you know. But then, how scared we were then, you can't imagine."

(No, wait. Here it is nonetheless, a tail to grab hold of: the mouse's tail, the mouse, the mouse puppet, puppet theater, they'll all sit in the living room and laugh, they'll make popcorn even, in a big pot with a glass lid, and watch it pop. And on Fridays they'll go out to eat in a restaurant, this will be their weekly treat, and Ariella, she'll order . . .)

"And all around—fog! Fog like you've never seen before! And I'm carried away on this raft in one direction, and Jimbo in the boat, who knows where he is. And I called out to Jimbo. But quietly, so the police won't hear. And he, like an idiot, he screams back to me . . ."

(. . . and ice cream for dessert. And when she grows up a bit, Galit, he'll be one of those fathers who embarrass their children at restaurants. Joking with the waitress, and when she asks how this or that dish tasted, he'll tell her honestly. And Galit, she'll say, ugh, Dad! Can't go out with you anywhere! And that's just the beginning. At class parties he'll volunteer to supervise, he'll sit in the kitchen with one of the other fathers, and from time to time stick his head through the door, are you behaving nicely, children? And Galit will no longer say ugh, Dad! nothing, just her face will say, c'mon, you're embarrassing me, go, go away already! And he'll return to the kitchen, and the two of them sitting there will say, how they've grown! How they've grown! I remember like it was yesterday . . .)

"And in the end I get there, totally wet, feeling like I swam from here to Nahariya, who knows how long it took, maybe ten minutes, but then it felt like a week to me. Climb onto the boat and what do I find? Jimbo sitting there asleep, got tired of looking for me, poor guy, definitely thought I drowned and was done for. And me, after I wring out my wet shirt, I say to him, Jimbo, Jimbo, what, you fell asleep? And he wakes up, did he ever wake up, jumps, almost cap- sized the boat on us, and he hugs me, says to me . . ."

(And so too at the end of high school. He'll sit there, in the crowd, with a camera—and rejoice. When she graduates college he'll no longer embarrass her. She'll understand him, understand the not-at-all-simple position of fathers in this world. And how he'll cry when she gets married! He and Ariella will each help hold the *chuppah*.)

"No, seriously, I'm telling you. For sure you dreamed it. Fog on the Yarkon? Whoever heard of such a thing. Thanks for worrying about me in your dream too, I joke. And he nods like this, thinking. We sit like that in silence for a minute or two and then suddenly his eyes stop on my shoes. Wait, he says to me. If I only dreamed it, where did your wet shoes come from? I thought I was going to piss from laughing, but he didn't laugh. Just said to me, you wouldn't do a thing like that . . ."

(They'll be the best grandfather and grandmother in the world, that's clear. There will be a cupboard full of sweets at home, and the grandchildren will be allowed to stay up until late, to jump rope in the living room, to eat in front of the television, to play with the computer until two in the morning even.)

"I was a boy, you understand? I didn't think he'd be so insulted. I thought, all told, we'd laugh a little."

(And in the shed, in a crate, after their death she'll find the doll, the curtains, and will remember that she had wonderful parents. Wonderful.)

"So I went there and apologized to him, I nearly kissed his black feet. And even today it bothers me, burns me here in my heart, because I work in a prison, you know, and every day hear about horrible, ugly acts, but this ugly act of mine, I swear, up till today, I still don't forgive myself for it."

"Uh huh," says Motti.

"Yeah, well," the Guard clears his throat. "That's how it was. Hard to believe, huh?"

"Uh huh."

"You wouldn't believe the sorts of things that happened afterward," says Guard B and hesitates. "You wouldn't believe them, I'm telling you. But I've got to go now, excuse me," he's embarrassed. "Remind me sometime, I'll tell you everything," he says, as if trying to salvage his dignity, to cover up the insult, for he's tried to put his life in someone else's hands, and was refused.

46

Daddy, Daddy, Galit will say when they stand on the porch and raise their arms to sky, or David will say, if it's a boy. Daddy, Daddy, the stars are so high! And Motti will say, right. They're way up high. And Galit or David will say, yes! Way up high! And will add in a serious and responsible voice, way up high! But not allowed without Daddy and Mommy!

He and Ariella will smile at each other above the head of the boy or the girl. Right, they'll say. But not allowed without Daddy and Mommy. And they'll hug and raise him or her up into the air, hup, hup, and give them a big, exciting spin around and around.

He'll never sit alone in his home with weak arms, veins drawn out under his skin in terminal blue, and hearing the door open ask, alarmed, who is it, who is it, I'm calling the police, who's there, who? Not like that. Because if the door is opened, when it's opened, certainly it will only be to admit people dear to his heart. He'll never fall in the street, trip over a stone sticking out in the sidewalk (someone, man or woman, will hold his hand, they'll walk with him calmly, they won't be impatient, won't make an issue of their ability to still move freely, won't make an issue of their still-flexible limbs). He won't sit alone—immersed in the shadows of his fading vision—on a street bench, longing for some passerby to ask him, need some help, Gramps? He won't sit there, fearing the rough voice, the rough hands that will grab his bag, that will rummage through his clothes to take his wallet. Won't try to string together a hopeless conversation with a nurse at the HMO office, a clerk at the post office or the national insurance, a receptionist, a telemarketer. If he suddenly wants to talk, to tell about his memories even (to leave them in someone's hands, so they won't be lost when he dies), if this is what he'll want, his loved ones will be with him to listen, to chat, to talk about things that happened, to ask his advice, perhaps even to laugh together. Way up high! he'll remember and tell them and they'll smile together. Way up high! But not allowed without Daddy and Mommy!

He toils over his love as others toil over the construction of a ship in a bottle. They have a whole table with lots of tweezers and small glue bottles and fine brushes. And the tweezers, this one is for the boards of the deck and this one is for the little sail, this one is to pull tight the ropes that will raise the sails and then the ship will sail, but where will it sail to, sealed in a bottle, that's not a problem, just seal it with a cork and throw it into the sea, such adventures await there.

47

I took them yesterday, said Menachem.

Fine fine, said Edna, who's already late for work. So take them today, too. You already know the way.

Very funny, said Menachem and didn't laugh. It's your turn today, c'mon. I'm late too.

What's this with my turn today? Edna got angry. This is a home here, not an amusement park. There's no line for rides. And where are you late to anyway? I swear.

The way you talk, you'd think that I just sit around here all day, Menachem got angry. It's going to take all day to finish this project. I'm already late anyway.

C'mon, said Edna, and I'm not late?

(Daddy, Daddy, said Avi. Look what I painted! Very nice, sweetie, said Menachem without looking.)

Edna repeated again, And I'm not late, Menachem?

If you got up early you wouldn't be late now. Menachem was annoyed. My day is organized to the minute. You know that. You'd think that I . . .

I'd think that you what? asked Edna. And Menachem answered, you'd think that I do this for the fun of it. I'm trying to support us here.

And what am I doing, excuse me? Edna asked angrily.

Don't start with me now, said Menachem. You know very well what I meant. And when we organized the days for driving . . .

When we organized the days for driving, Edna interrupted him, we organized them like that so it would be convenient for the both of us. And today isn't convenient for me. This isn't a contract with a lawyer here, Menachem, she said and swept her keys, wallet, and cell phone into her purse.

What a shame, said Menachem.

Really a shame, Edna said angrily. Because then I would insert a clause, the signee is prohibited from being a lazy ass who isn't even willing to take his children to daycare.

Don't make this into more than what it is, said Menachem.

I'm not making this into anything whatsoever, said Edna. They're your children too, you know. You're always complaining that you don't spend enough time with them, so here, you got more time. Now just do me a favor and take them and that's all, okay?

Fine, fine, said Menachem and got up from the table, finishing the rest of his coffee in one gulp and then making a face because of the grounds. But you owe me.

Sure thing, said Edna. Okay, I'm off.

Give us a kiss, said Menachem.

She gave.

Daddy, asked one of the children, are we going already?

We're going already, answered Menachem, who was still getting dressed in the bedroom.

Daddy, can you make me a sandwich?

We're already late, said Menachem, who returned to the kitchen and tied his shoes.

But I'm hungry.

We'll buy you something on the way, said Menachem. Let's go, let's go, late already.

Daddy, can we do piggyback to the car?

Not today, said Menachem and grabbed the keys. It's already very late.

They got into the car and drove off.

Daddy, his son Avi asked him when they arrived at daycare, do you miss Grandpa?

Of course, said Menachem.

I miss him too, said Avi.

That's great, said Menachem and closed the car door.

And after he left the kids at daycare, after he returned home and peeked into the secret box and sat down to work, he didn't know that, in another ten years (ten years from now), his daughter would come home hurt and with filthy pants, and straight from the shower would get into bed, and wouldn't leave it for maybe two days, and regardless, now he was wasting time answering emails and surfing back and forth between news sites, and in spite of this he still managed to finish the project, his insufficient time was nevertheless enough, and he forgot to go out with Laika, but she held on until evening. Good girl.

48

And this is how you teach a dog to heel:

First, make the dog like you and gain his confidence. This is easy: one can inundate him with treats. One can play with him, pet him, scratch him behind the ears, go to scary places and protect him there.

Now attach a leash to his collar. There are those who use a choke collar. They use them immediately, with every dog, whether it's needed or not, just to cause pain. We won't concern ourselves with such people. Right away they pull forcefully, so the dog will obey out of fear. This is certainly the easy, faster way. Results right away—though others will pay the price. We have no interest in this.

Go out with your leash. With your dog at its end. And treats, of course. Especially treats. And teach him, the dog, to come to you. Call him joyfully, almost ecstatically. Come here! Good dog! Come, come, come! Wanna come here? Come here, good dog! Good dog!

Call him with longing. And when he comes (before this you can give a light tug on the leash—just to get his attention, not to cause pain), praise and pet him. And again a treat. Lots of treats. The dog doesn't understand where they come from. Just enjoys the taste, the smell, our giving. *Inundate* them, this is a key word. Inundate.

Afterward, walk. And the dog walks as well. The leash is slack. And when the dog goes in another direction, when he walks away from us, pull the leash. Turn your back to him, tug on the leash, and quickly let go. Don't hurt him. It's unpleasant nevertheless. Turn your back to him so he won't know that we're pulling. So he won't connect the pulling to us, and if he makes the connection, he won't see your hand giving it away. He'll only connect it to his walking away from us. And when he comes close, when he gets to us, another treat. Good dog! What a good dog! We're surprised he came to us. He's not surprised by our surprise. He doesn't know that we pulled.

And likewise in this manner, again and again. And then—heel. Sit him down right next to your leg. It's not hard to teach him to sit. Part of a treat next to his nose, lift it up (sit!), and when his eyes follow it his head is pulled, following his gaze, upward. It's not comfortable to stand this way, and he sits down. Good dog! Again, good dog!

Sit him right next to your leg, say heel, then start walking. Heel! Heel! Good dog. And if he turns his eyes or walks away, again a quick tug on the leash. Let go immediately. Never any tension in the leash. Leave it almost always slack. And when he's with us again, right next to your leg, good dog! Good dog! Heel, good dog! Like that, in a cheerful voice, so he'll be happy. Good dog! Good dog!

And continue to walk. From time to time a treat (you can also hold it in front of his snout, tucked inside your hand for example, so the dog will follow it, good dog!). And like that again and again. And petting, a lot of petting and praise. And when he turns his head or walks away—the leash. Walk in straight lines. Turn at right angles and say, heel. And the leash. And treats as well. And praise. A lot of praise. So walking next to us will be a positive experience, the promise of wonderful things.

Rest from time to time. The dog loses focus. Resting too is a prize: when he walks well, close to us and absolutely attentive, surprise him with, Go on, boy! Run free! Good dog! And play, jump and play, rest together, get something to drink. And back to work. Work together. And if the dog gets very tired, that's the time to teach him to lie down. It's very hard for them to learn this. They learn quickly, but with great effort. There is some internal resistance: lying down is a position of great submissiveness. Therefore, if they refuse at some point after already learning it, tug on the leash again. A sharp tug, so they'll lie down immediately. And let go quickly. But not this time. Not yet. Now we're still waiting for exhaustion. Exhaustion is on our side. The desire to rest will already be associated with the desire to satisfy, with treats, with praise. Good dog! Good dog! Run free, good dog!

49

Hey man, Menachem said on the phone.

Hi, said Motti.

Laika's fine, said Menachem. It's a little unpleasant for Menachem, remembering the way he behaved last time. On the one hand, two in the morning is just not the time to make a call. On the other, the man is rotting in jail for him, and to be woken up by a phone call, well, it's not exactly comparable, that debt and this one. What's more, Motti (Menachem thinks) has plenty of justification for acting a bit strange. What, it's not strange to go to prison for someone? Strange.

Yes, continued Menachem. Plays with the kids and all. You have nothing to worry about, okay? We're taking good care of her for you.

That's great, said Motti. Thanks a lot. Say hi to Edna, too.

Of course, of course, said Menachem. Listen, why am I calling? Because I just wanted to apologize, because today's Wednesday and I'm not coming.

That's all right, said Motti. You told me last week. You have a family and all, I know that it doesn't always work out.

Don't make me laugh, man, said Menachem. You know you're number one with me, right? Just don't tell Edna. You're number one. In any case, what did I want to tell you?

I don't know, said Motti. You still haven't said.

Exactly, said Menachem. I wanted to say that I'm not coming today, because tomorrow we're going on a vacation for a few days with the kids, it's Edna who insisted, women, you know how it is.

Of course, of course, said Motti, though he didn't know at all.

Yeah, confirmed Menachem. But next week I'm there on time, okay? And don't worry about the dog. She's staying here at the house, but the neighbors' son will come to play with her every day and take her on a walk, too. He's a good kid, you can trust him. I'm paying him, just so you know.

As long as he'll be careful with her, said Motti and his heart sunk a bit. Nothing will happen to her, right?

I told you that I trust him, said Menachem. He's a good kid, I'm telling you.

But he'll be careful with her, repeated Motti.

Of course he'll be careful, of course, said Menachem, and anyone listening closely would have perhaps recognized a slight hint of impatience in his voice, because my God, him and his stupid dog, I mean really.

So okay, said Motti. Have a good time there, say hi to the kids too.

Of course, of course, said Menachem. What's with you? You managing?

Of course, Motti said too. There's a, uh, there's a pretty good library here. They bring us movies, too.

Right on, you got a real film festival there, huh, said Menachem. Having fun, huh? You keep it up like that and I'll stop showing up at all, he joked.

50

And then he put down the phone and returned to the table. Who was that, asked Edna. No one, he answered.

Tomorrow I'll bring the kids to daycare, Edna said. And he said, thanks.

And Edna left the room, maybe she went to fry up eggs for the kids, maybe a frittata.

What are you looking at, he asked Laika, who was curled up next to his chair. She didn't answer.

He started working, but his concentration wasn't the best.

What are you making, he yelled to the kitchen.

An omelet, she called.

Make me one too?

Edna didn't answer.

Make me one too?

Of course, of course, said Edna. You don't have to ask for everything twice.

Okay, okay, answered Menachem, but very quietly. What are you so mad about.

Can you come help me for a second, Edna called.

Just a sec, said Menachem.

Never mind, said Edna a moment later. And another moment later said, come on, the food's ready.

Start without me, said Menachem. I'm busy with something.

It's getting cold, Edna said.

So I'll eat it cold, said Menachem. Go ahead and eat. I'm coming in a second.

Should I bring it to you there, asked Edna.

No need, said Menachem. Thanks.

I'll cover it up for you, said Edna.

And after some time Menachem took a break from whatever it was that he was busy with, came to the empty table, and ate a cold omelet. And a slice of bread. And then returned to his desk. There's a lot to do.

The kids want to say goodnight to you, Edna called out.

I'll be there in a sec, said Menachem.

And after a few minutes, maybe twenty, Edna came to him. Okay, they're already sleeping, she said. Everything all right with you?

Of course it's all right, said Menachem. Why wouldn't it be all right?

Don't know, said Edna. No reason.

And she left the room. Probably went to watch TV. After some time the phone rang, and she answered in the other room, and after two or three minutes came back in to Menachem. Your dad's on the phone, she said. Answer quick, it's a collect call.

Tell him I'm not home, said Menachem and turned back to the desk.

He's calling from South America, reminded Edna.

Tell him I'm not home, repeated Menachem.

He knows you're here, I told him. C'mon, what's with you, she asked.

So tell him I'm in the bathroom, said Menachem impatiently.

Edna shrugged. Have it your way, she said.

She left, and after a time returned, and asked, you coming to bed?

In just a moment I'll be done here, said Menachem.

Okay, said Edna. I'm already exhausted.

Don't wait up for me, said Menachem. It'll take me a little more time here.

Goodnight, said Edna.

Goodnight, said Menachem.

51

And the routine as well. Oh, the wondrous routine, thinks Motti, who's already nodding off on his thin mattress, on the tightly stretched bedding, he turns onto his side and forces his way up against the cold wall. He'll leave for work in the morning, maybe he'll go back to being a teacher, Ariella will be a meteorologist even or a receptionist or a plastic surgeon. He'll have to leave for work in the morning, before then he'll wake up (he's almost asleep now), he'll wake up a few minutes before her and bring her a cup of coffee in bed, every morning he'll bring her a cup of coffee in bed, they'll barely exchange a word, they won't be morning people, they'll just wander around the space of their house gathering up their bags, wallets, children even, they'll wander around still half asleep, they'll grab a little something to eat, before this he'll wait next to the bathroom door for her to finish getting ready, he'll go in to shower, to get dressed, Ariella, he'll yell to her, did you see my shoes, and she'll say, silly, you left them next to the sofa in front of the TV, you fell asleep like a rock last night, I could barely wake you to get you to bed, and he'll trudge over to the living room and indeed, there are his shoes, he'll mumble something, yeah, here they are, and they'll both leave for work. At lunch he'll call her, hi sweetie, it's me, did you get to work? Everything okay? And she'll say, I've been here two hours already, silly, I already sewed up two patients or I forecasted a hurricane or scattered showers, and he'll say, that's wonderful, I'm running to class, we'll talk later, see you at home. And they will, they'll actually see each other at home, they'll prepare dinner together, eat it at the table in the kitchen, it's covered in Formica, or in the living room watching television, they'll watch the news and she'll say, that's terrible, that's terrible, and he'll hug her and say, but our lives are good, right? And it's because of you that our lives are good. And on holidays they'll take trips abroad, and at night she'll say, it's fun like this, just you and me, like it used to be, before the kids. And he'll say, yes, yes, he'll say it and look into her eyes by the light of the candle on the table of the small restaurant, across the checkered tablecloth, the empty plates, the nearly empty bottle of wine, he'll say yes, yes, and enter her, they're in bed in a clean but not pricey hotel, and they'll fall asleep hugging afterward, no, she'll fall asleep and he'll stay awake a few more minutes, as he does every night, to look at her and caress her hair, and she'll murmur adorably in her sleep, and then he'll fall asleep, too.

"Anyway," continues Guard B, who now glances right and left along the corridor and then sits down with a dull thud next to the door of Motti's cell, continuing as if days hadn't passed since he last stopped his story, as if he doesn't know that Motti has already fallen asleep (and in truth he doesn't know), "Me and Tom are standing there across from the prison building—the detention center, actually—and he says, come, we're going to free Jimbo. And I said, what, with a lawyer and all that? And he said to me, what are you talking about, we'll smuggle a spoon inside like in the movies, and he'll dig himself a tunnel out! That will definitely take him a million years, I told him. Everything's cement, all the walls and stuff, and by the time he finishes digging they'll already have him on the plane and that's that. Maybe a lawyer is still worth it? And Tom says to me, listen, you don't know anything about life, you. Whoever heard of a prisoner who gets out with a lawyer? We'll steal sheets and tear up strips, we'll make a rope ladder out of them and we'll bake a pie, and he'll write a prison diary like revolutionary heroes write, about his lost freedom and his oppressed brethren and all that, and when we finish it all we'll be heroes of freedom and our pictures will be in all the papers! But Tom, I said to him, isn't it simpler to get money for bail? Maybe we could just go to your aunt and we'll tell her . . . but he said, what's the sense in that? He'll make a digging tool, make it out of a teaspoon, maybe he'll sharpen it on his bed or something, and then we'll break him out of there, a real daring operation, we'll all climb down together on the ropes that we'll tie badly right to the bars, we'll do everything by the glare of the searchlights with all the alarms and the dogs barking—there was only one dog there, I can tell you, and he was old, too, and there was no more than one searchlight at most—and then maybe the rope will unravel, that would be the best, and one of us will fall and break a leg and then limp away to freedom. Maybe even sacrifice himself for the sake of his comrades' liberty. But maybe, I suggested to him, maybe instead of that we could cut the fence when he goes out to the courtyard and then we'll slip him out through the hole? And Tom said, c'mon, really! It's clear you got no education, you. That's two minutes of work, that's all—what kind of escape is that? And I sneezed then, I got pneumonia and go figure what else from that swim in the Yarkon by the time they caught us. I couldn't stop sneezing and then coughing, I almost choked, we went away quickly before they caught us looking, even though with the workforce trouble, I'm telling you, it's a miracle they even had time to count the prisoners. We agreed to take a little break from our adventure, so Tom went home and me to the health clinic. Two or three days later I was like new, you know? And the doctor who took care of me, he's still my doctor, and if I'll have kids, he'll be their doctor too."

52

C'mon, said Edna to Menachem a few days later, are you coming to bed already, Fatty?

What'd you call me? Menachem straightened up in his chair.

What? Fatty? repeated Edna.

Menachem got up from his chair and then stood there thinking, rubbing his belly, which had started to swell.

C'mon, what are you making a big deal about? said Edna. You may be a fatty, but you're my fatty. Come to bed already, I swear. I'm half dead from exhaustion.

I'm coming, I'm coming, said Menachem. It really grew, my gut, huh?

A little, said Edna. It doesn't bother me.

So I should probably start exercising a little, huh? said Menachem and patted it. A man needs to watch himself.

Do what you want, said Edna. If you think you'll enjoy it, why not.

Menachem rubbed his neck with an aching hand. I have to start running or something, huh? Just have to.

Do what you want, repeated Edna, but how about later. Come to bed already, c'mon. Fatty.

That's Mr. Fatty to you, said Menachem, like it was a line from a sitcom. And I'm coming to bed—he raised his voice, but only very, very slightly, so as not to wake the children—I'm coming to bed, and I'll crush you, look out!

Edna giggled like a young girl. I know how to take care of myself, Mr. Fatty. Don't threaten me. Just hurry, I'm already falling asleep standing up.

They went and he crushed. Edna turned over satisfied and fell asleep immediately. Menachem was still thinking: Tomorrow after work I'm buying running shoes.

So, how was it? Asked Edna when he came back sweating and let Laika loose into the space of their living room.

Hard, motherfucker, said Menachem, but I feel awesome. We ran up to the big intersection and circled half the neighborhood.

Way to go, said Edna, who was already back to cutting vegetables for a salad.

Yeah, said Menachem. But a little difficult with what's her name, Laika. Every second she wants to stop and sniff.

Teach her to heel, suggested Edna.

Sure, said Menachem, and slumped down on the armchair.

And don't flop down on the chairs like that, added Edna, who heard the springs creaking. At least change your shirt.

I'm hitting the shower in a second, said Menachem and massaged his knees.

Great, said Edna. Food will be ready in ten more minutes. Come here, Laika, she said to Laika, who stared at her. Who wants some carrot? Who wants some? Who's my sweetie? Go ahead! Laika gently took the carrot and hid it in her secret cache in the folds of the armchair in the living room. Immediately returned to ask for more, and got it, too.

The next day Menachem took advantage of his lunch break in order to head over to a nearby mall. I need to teach a dog to run with me, he said to a salesman at the pet store. Teach her to heel? asked the salesman, his cell phone still in one hand and his girlfriend waiting on the line. Yeah, super, said Menachem. Wait a sec, sweetie, the salesman had brought his cell phone back to his ear. I'll call you back in another minute, okay sweetie? Me too. Me too. No, you first. No, you first. Okay, together, he winked to Menachem. One, two, and . . . hung up. Here, he said to Menachem. Choke collar. Exactly what you need. Put it on her. If she doesn't go with you, give a good pull once or twice. They learn real quick with these. Is she a big dog?

Bigger than life, said Menachem. Pack it up for me quick, okay, buddy? I need to get back to work.

He packed it up for him quick. And in the evening Menachem came home full of energy, a decision is a decision, changed clothes just like that and put on the new shoes. Laika, come here! He called. Let's go for a walk!

And Laika came. He put the jangling collar on her, connected the leash, and out they went. When she stopped to sniff, he pulled hard. Started to run, pulled again, and her after him. Did she have a choice? They ran. From time to time, whenever she dawdled, he pulled. And when he stopped at the big intersection to tighten his laces, he bent down and put the leash under his foot. Laika now pulled back, one quick pull. Hup, she freed herself. Right into the street she ran. The truck was already approaching fast. Menachem looked away.

When he looked back, Laika was no longer there. The truck continued on its way, the street empty. At night the driver of the truck went home and took off his shoes and his wife made him a cup of tea. Laika! called Menachem. Laika! Come here, Laika!

Laika didn't come. And why should she come. He continued searching for her. And for another night or two after this as well. Edna searched too, and said, maybe she'll come back on her own. Maybe she'll go back to Motti's place, let's swing by there, take a look. But Laika didn't return. Not on those nights and not on any others.

Menachem called Motti. And Motti was called from his cell to the phone. And Menachem said to him, I don't know how it happened, believe me. One moment she's there, the next I don't see her.

Motti's legs failed him. Not the way they write in books, "his legs failed him," did they fail. I mean, they truly failed. Went out from under him. He tried to suck in some air but there was something stuck in his throat, something large, very large, nothing went out and nothing came in. His knees now on the cold floor and the guard looking at him, astonished, perhaps concerned, hurrying to put a kind hand on his shoulder, to calm him, but Motti, what does he have to do with him. Just a whimper escaped and he collapsed, his hands went to his face, then fell shaking to his chest, returned shaking to his face. As if his body was trying to draw itself inward, to fill up the terrible hole. And he was surprised that all his bodily functions were still functioning, more or less. That is to say, breathing, sweating, the pressure in his bladder, even his nails grew a bit; only the beats of his broken heart were affected, were quickened, it was certainly possible to hear them on the other end of the telephone line. Motti thought he would die, but nevertheless knelt there next to the phone, the floor cold and the hand of the guard warm, and nevertheless went on breathing, his internal systems continued to function normally, all in all, and this is just more proof that even an unbearable pain can be born.

You lost her? (Motti almost wailed, almost vomited.) You lost my dog? When I get out of here I'll kill you, Menachem. Do you hear me? When I get out of here I'll kill you.

Go ahead, go ahead, you piece of shit, Menachem screamed now, he suddenly erupted, who do you think you're threatening? Shut your mouth, you fuck, you weirdo, or I'll come out there and tear you a new one.

54

"So that's it," said Guard B. "That's my life. That's my story, that's what happened. That's it. Sometimes I still ask myself what happened to them, to everyone. Where they are now. Where's Jimbo, where's the aunt, the widow, old Sammy Clemens . . . Like, where are they, you know? For sure you've found yourself thinking about that here a lot, too, huh? All day long just sitting and thinking, what else is there to do here. Just thinking where is everyone now."

And Motti, sitting in his cell, and all this was already days, months, maybe two or three years later, his eyes are already dry, asked where is she now, really. He asked himself. And an entirely new door suddenly opened up to him. The where is she now door. We thought there was no limit, this head of his goes everywhere, these stories run everywhere, but where is she now, actually? With the wolf packs, the wild dogs, wandering around the city, and it's good for her, so very good. Wandering sometimes around the prison walls and waiting for him. And then that other one, asleep in bed, mouth open a bit, a bit of children's saliva accumulating on her pillow. Sits with her parents in the living room and watches television. Hides behind the sofa, she's not allowed to be awake at this hour, and in spite of this she's in the living room, sitting behind her parents and watching television. Packs a bag for tomorrow, spreads a slice of bread, peels a cucumber. Does homework. Falls asleep to music playing, a girl band or a boy band, things that you listen to at that age. Opens a book. Sleeps nevertheless. Crouches over the toilet. Throws a tennis ball against the wall and catches it, then throws it again. Brushes her teeth. Pets a cat. Showers. (He imagines only the youthful silhouette from the other side of the curtain. No, not even that. Just the sound of the water from the other side of the door.) Places the clothes for tomorrow already folded on a chair, she's such a good girl. Sits at the table at the house of a friend from school, eating French fries with their hands, dipping them in ketchup, sprinkling salt, gulping down juice with an intense color. ("And then I remember—did I tell you this already? Stop me if I did, but suddenly I recall, I recall the two of us, me and Tom, how we hid there in the thicket and watched everyone," laughs Guard B. Motti isn't listening to him.) Cries, maybe she got hit. Cleans her ears with a cotton swab. Argues with Mom. With Dad. Tennis ball against the wall, catches again, throws again. At a class party, a bottle spins in a circle, all the kids are giggling. At home, asleep for some time already. At a class party, in a closed closet, seven minutes in heaven, she and a boy. No. Yes, in spite of this in a closed closet, she and a boy, breathing heavily and outside everyone laughs, and he puts his hand under (no) (yes, he puts his hand under) he puts his hand under her shirt, the two of them hold their breath, enough, c'mon, she's asleep in bed, and the saliva accumulates . . . but no, at a party nevertheless, in a closet, and the boy, the hand, the shirt, there's still nothing there, nothing has sprouted there, she's just a kid, c'mon, enough of this, enough of this, with the jealousy and with, c'mon, she's just a kid and what does it matter anyway, no, it's not jealousy, something else now, what is it, doesn't matter, no, she's definitely sleeping now anyway, nothing has sprouted there yet, chest flat like a boy's, and the hand, c'mon, the breath, enough already with all of this, enough with this already, a tightly closed fist into the wall, anything not to cry, even hitting the wall this way like a spoiled boy, c'mon, boy, enough, enough with this, enough already, his knuckles hurt him, but how do you cut off this flow of thoughts, how do you cut it off.

55

And after they slept together at Motti's place, right in his bed, after he entered her from behind and they moaned and then lay back down and then went up and down like children playing, slowly and then quickly, very, very quickly, after all this she got up and went to the bathroom and he, Menachem, remained resting and fixed his eyes on the ceiling. Make some room for me, too, said Sigal when she returned to the bed. (He didn't cheat on Edna again after this, it was a one-time thing, or nearly one time, and Motti's apartment is empty, where else could he bring her, he has a key, it was bound to happen, and anyway he was already there a few days earlier, the downstairs neighbors called because of the leak, he arrived to open up for the plumber, because Motti or no Motti, he still has the key, suddenly the urge to stay there after him, after the plumber, to stay there alone, but he didn't stay, no, paid in cash, didn't even take a receipt, left and locked up, descended the stairs together, each man went on his way, and a few days afterwards Sigal and everything, well the apartment's empty, and Edna, what she doesn't know can't hurt her, and she won't know, she'll never know, and after all the years that will stretch out from this point he too will almost forget that all of this ever was.)

Hugged her, that doesn't cost him anything, suddenly thought about Edna and the kids, perhaps twitched a bit, Sigal didn't feel a thing though her head rested on his right arm. After some time she smiled at him, they were silent, she got up and put her clothes back on, it was clear to her as well that nothing would ever come of this, he never considered telling her, I'll leave my wife for you, he never even thought to lie like that, nor did she expect it.

All right, I'm off, she said to him finally. Uh, and the toilet won't flush.

I know, Menachem got up, too. It's because of the plumber, with the faucet. Need to wait for it to dry.

I once went out with a plumber, said Sigal. Now why did I tell you that? she laughed. I'm like that, don't know how to keep my mouth shut.

It's okay, said Menachem. Okay bye, said Sigal and kissed him on his cheek.

Bye, said Menachem too.

Closed the door after her and wandered around the apartment. In the morning he argued a bit with Edna (don't you raise your voice with me, she screamed at him as if his voice was a big stick and he was lifting it up, high into the air, and threatening her), now he's there alone, in the evening he'll be home again and they'll make up.

Paced around the apartment. Where is it, he asked himself. Where is it, Motti's father box? Went from room to room, lost interest, went into the bathroom and stood over the toilet, when he finished he reached his hand out for the handle, remembered not to, drew it back, zipped up, washed his hands. In the bedroom he spread out the sheets that were covered in dust and the dust that covered them had already been disturbed. Out of habit he opened up the refrigerator, it's empty, would have been better if it was left open in the first place, it's a haven for mold. Put on his shoes, the windows are closed, turned off the lights, got out, locked up.

56

The time passed and more time came and it too passed. Eyes dried again and observed the ceiling. And they were telling him to leave, well, everything was regulated to begin with, and when he left the cell for the last time Guard B escorted him on the long walk down the lit, the well-lit, whitewashed corridors. "Think," Guard B said to him, "all these years of your life because of alcohol, damn it." "Yes," said Motti. "My father also drank a lot," Guard B said to him. They walked and walked. "Did I tell you that already?" "You told me," said Motti. "Alcoholic," sighed Guard B. "Tried to quit once, tried a thousand times. Would throw out everything in the house, some house, would empty everything into the sink, throw the key out the window, some window, last a day, last two days, in the end he'd crack. He'd always find something in the end. Once drank a bottle of aftershave. Threw it all up."

Motti stopped. This is the bridge, this is the bridge, he thought. Sayings, bastardized sayings—language is the bridge, these are the bridges to him. "The chins of the fathers shall be visited upon their sons, huh?" he tried.

Guard B look at him, amazed. "Not at all, he never visited me again after that," he said.

"Of course he didn't," said Motti and closed his eyes for a moment. "Of course he didn't."

And they had already arrived at the entrance, and Guard B put a hand on Motti's shoulder, in spite of everything he put it there, no one said a thing, they stood like this another moment, oh my, look, look at them, at all the people in this novel, almost all of them, if someone would really hug them, if someone held them tight, they'd fall to pieces.

"Keep in touch, yeah?" Guard B said to him. "Give me a call, I'm in the book."

The phone book, that is.

57

Sarah Rosenthal Sarah Rosenthal Sarah Rosenthal. Sarah Rosenthal of blessed memory. Of blessed memory. Sarah Rosenthal, may God avenge her. Sorely missed. Woe is us for we have been broken the crown of our head is fallen the righteous Sarah Rosenthal. A gentle woman pure of heart. Sarah Rosenthal may her virtue protect us. Here lies Sarah Rosenthal. Sarah Rosenthal born Hebrew date passed away Hebrew date fell in the course of duty. Taken from us before her time who will console us. Sarah Rosenthal passed away Hebrew date daughter of Puah and Moshe oh grief and bitter wailing. The precious woman Sarah Rosenthal Sarah Rozenthal. Rozental. Sarah Rosenthal beloved mother loyal daughter loved the beauty of the land. Sarah blasphemous writing Rosenthal a swastika sprayed in paint. Sarah Rosenthal the writing hard to read. Sarah Rosenthal a quote from an Amichai poem loved and was loved. Here lies Sarah Rosenthal a woman of valor and an inspiration to all. Sweet in her ways, observant in her good deeds. Sarah Rosenthal gone but not forgotten. God-fearing Sarah Rosenthal of blessed memory. Sarah Rosenthal daughter wife of, sister to, mother. Modest was she Sarah Rosenthal blessed among women. Princes have persecuted me without a cause but my heart stands in awe of thy word, consider my affliction and deliver me for I do not forget thy Torah, teach me O Lord the way of thy statutes and I shall keep it to the end. Here (here) lies Sarah Rosenthal. Here she lies.

FOURTH

OUTSIDE

The familiar physiognomy of a word, the feeling that it has taken up its meaning into itself, that it is an actual likeness of its meaning—there could be human beings to whom all this was alien. (They would not have an attachment to their words.)—And how are these feelings manifested among us?—By the way we choose and value words.

How do I find the "right" word? How do I choose among words? Without doubt it is sometimes as if I were comparing them by fine differences of smell: *That* is too . . . . . . , *that* is too . . . . . . , —*this* is the right one.—But I do not always have to make judgments, give explanations; often I might only say: "It simply isn't right yet." I am dissatisfied, I go on looking. At last a word comes: "*That's* it!" *Sometimes* I can say why. This is simply what searching, this is what finding, is like here.

—Ludwig Wittgenstein, *Philosophical Investigations*

58

Menachem continued to pay the property tax, even though they hadn't spoken since. Perhaps only two or three times, awkwardly. And no one had been in the apartment for years. He cleaned it quite well before he left, even the stale air will dissipate after a night or two with the windows open (it will return to the global cycle, atoms commingling with atoms, molecules with molecules and so on). Motti closes the refrigerator door and plugs it back in. He puts a sealed bottle of water he bought specially in the freezer, a bottle that he bought on the way over. For two years he didn't have really cold water. In the morning he'll be surprised to find it didn't freeze. He'll open the bottle, drink a bit, choke on the cold for a moment. In the instant that its lid is unsealed, when the outside is let in, frost will spread throughout the water, from top to bottom all of it will be colored pale white. Many things wait until a place is found for them. The sight is so beautiful, beautiful and private and surprising. Motti will not share it with anyone.

In any case, he urinated, the toilet doesn't flush, some kind of residue there, and what sort of way is this for characters to meet, it's totally pathetic, pardon me, turned on the faucet, the water ran and filled up the basin, he washed, again the water ran to fill up the basin, he sat a moment, showered, dressed, went out to the convenience store to buy food and toilet paper. And when he returned a young woman stood, beautiful as he imagined, in the entrance to the neighboring apartment. Ariella? They moved, said the new neighbor. Where did they move to? asked Motti. Don't know, said the new neighbor. They moved. Will you come over for coffee later? Meet Benjamin and the kids.

Went into his place and wandered through the rooms. Sat down in one and sat down in another, sat on the bed maybe half a minute, got up again, wandered around. In the end sat in the living room, put his ear again up close to the cold wall. Out of habit.

They say it's never too late to become someone else. And in another life he could have been a different person, only there isn't another life.

And do you know what? Perhaps in the end he did meet the grown-up, perfect Ariella, and she was everything he dreamed of, even more, and they had a life together, a good, long life, and they had children or didn't have children, in any event they raised many dogs and even traveled abroad regularly, maybe adopted a cat or two as well, performed good and important deeds, their days were full of joy, why not. In the end they died, of course. When you go on long enough, all stories end in death. But there could definitely be some sort of happy ending here, I promise. The problem is just knowing where to stop.

TRANSLATOR'S AFTERWORD

Israel is not the easiest place to live. Indeed, this country confronts its highly diverse population with a similarly varied set of difficulties. A very partial list includes national conflict, ethnic tension, and religious strife, all three of which are often described as intractable. But this almost unimaginable difficulty presents certain advantages to writers, even or especially writers of fiction. The world, after all, finds difficulty fascinating. At home and abroad people want to understand the difficulty that is Israel, want someone to give it all a name, want to read the words of a writer equipped to tie it all up with a poetic flourish. Readers from Korea to Brazil are searching for someone capable of positioning a few well-drawn individuals against that wide canvas of historical, political, social, and religious overabundance (also known as "the Conflict"), thereby making this overabundance a bit more intelligible. This is how the novel, as a genre, compensates for its fictional status, how it manages to constitute a form of knowledge despite never having happened: it takes the political and the historical and translates them into the personal and the biographical so that the individual reader can finally understand.

The global desire to understand this bottomless difficulty is remarkable. There are seven million people in Israel (depending on how you count—even the straightforward matter of counting inhabitants is far from simple over there), which is roughly the same number of people who live in Bulgaria or Honduras. But how many of their writers get translated into English? In the last twenty years over five hundred book-length works from Hebrew literature have been published in English.[1]

But this worldwide interest comes with strings attached. People read Hebrew writers primarily to get The Story. The big one. The national one. Or the religious-cum-national one. People read for the epic story, the one with all those wars fought over and against that possibly mystical two-thousand-year-old backdrop. Israeli writers can be critical, their stories can be ironic, tragic even, so long as they include The Story.

In this regard the book before you disappoints, or, more accurately, disobeys. Take Asaf Schurr's *Motti*, change the names of the main characters, switch around another fifty words scattered here and there, and delete, by my count, a single three-sentence stretch (describing a dream of all things), and this novel could be set in any of a thousand cities around the world. Unless I'm way, way off here (or unless you're one of those readers who thinks absolutely everything is an allegory[2]), I'd say that this book, despite the language

---

1   This figure—which includes fiction, poetry, and books for children—comes from Nilli Cohen at the Institute for the Translation of Hebrew Literature.

2   The influential Marxist critic Fredric Jameson has advanced such an approach to so-called "third-world" literature (an obviously problematic category, especially in the Israeli case). In "third-world texts," according to him, "the story of the private individual destiny is always an allegory of the embattled situation of the public third-world culture and society." Jameson's widely read article is typically rejected in scholarly circles, but I think it's fair to say this allegorical shadow looms over much reading of, in this case, modern Hebrew fiction. See

and country in which it was written, is not about Israel. It just isn't. This in itself is noteworthy. The very absence of Israel in this Israeli novel does tell us something about contemporary Israeli culture,[3] but contemplating the presence of this absence only takes us so far. To understand *Motti*, one must look elsewhere.

■

So what is *Motti* about? Plot summary won't really explain it. There's a man (Motti), a dog, a friend, an object of affection, an accident, and an extremely difficult (there's that word again) decision. Even for a short novel, not that much really happens. As such, some readers will dismiss *Motti* for failing to tell a conventional story (if they didn't already dismiss it for failing to tell The Story).

But this book most certainly should be understood as a novel, and a novel tapping into one of the genre's central traditions. *Motti* is a novel riddled with self-consciousness. Asaf Schurr—or Asaf Schurr as implied author—is everywhere in this book, reflecting on the story being told, interrupting the story no longer being told,

Fredric Jameson, "Third-World Literature in the Era of Multinational Capitalism," *Social Text*, No. 15 (Autumn, 1986), pp. 65–88.

3   It should be noted that *Motti* received considerable attention upon its publication in Israel, including a glowing front-page review in the *Haaretz* book supplement (more or less the Israeli equivalent of the *New York Times Book Review* or the *Guardian*). The Israeli reading public's (and/or its critical establishment's) readiness to accept and even embrace *Motti* on its own unconventional terms says something about the expansive sense of what constitutes Israeli culture within Israel here in the early twenty-first century. Anglophone reading sensibilities, I'm guessing, are rather parochial by comparison, as I'd more confidently recommend *Motti* to a fan of David Foster Wallace than to one who prefers Amos Oz.

and drawing attention to the contrived nature of the project of novel writing as a whole.

This approach to the form, this refusal to let the story simply be, this impulse to draw back the curtain, is a tradition stretching back to what may well have been the very first novel, Cervantes's *Don Quixote*. Unfortunately, the gradual resurgence and apparent ubiquity of this gesture during the last half century—following a longer stretch that included nineteenth-century realism, during which period this narrative strategy receded—has lead many people to mistake it as a recent (and thus trivial or frivolous) trend. Nowadays the self-conscious novel is often identified, categorized, and then dismissed as "postmodernist" (or, even worse, as "po-mo"), and that's that. Such thinking seems to believe that the "serious novel" and the "postmodernist novel" occupy mutually exclusive categories.

But identifying a strategy at work in a novel is not the same as explaining the meaning of either. In other words, not all self-conscious novels are created equal. Indeed, the technique is remarkably flexible, which explains, in part, why novelists have returned to it again and again throughout the genre's four-hundred-year history.

Motti is most certainly—to quote Robert Alter's description of the self-conscious novel in general—"the kind of novel that expresses its seriousness through playfulness."[4] Though even this may be overstating Schurr's interest in anything smacking of the antic. In contemporary American fiction, the appearance of the writer in his or her own plot, or even the mention of a third-person narra-

---

4   Robert Alter, *Partial Magic: The Novel as Self-Conscious Genre* (Berkeley: University of California Press, 1975), ix.

tor's self-awareness within a narrative, often operates as a distancing gesture. Through this move the writer flaunts a certain cleverness, demonstrates his or her mastery of the genre's many incarnations, or simply compels the reader to recognize the underlying absurdity of fully caring about this illusion we call fiction.

By contrast, Asaf Schurr employs this strategy with almost dead-pan candor. As I read it, this novel's many self-conscious asides seem the product of pure, unadorned honesty and sensitive, lucid contemplation. Put differently, this novel is in large part an oddly humble reflection on writing, on imagining a world, and on trying to make sense of our real world through an extended exercise that relies on nothing but words. Schurr's "playfulness" is perfectly sincere and thus raises the emotional stakes of the narrative. He might spoil the illusion that is his story, but this is a small price to pay for the multi-dimensional clarity and unlikely wonder this novel offers again and again. As he says at the end of his preface about the book to come, "everything is on the table and in midair the table stands."

I suspect that this tendency toward self-consciousness reflects one of Schurr's central motivations as a writer, but Schurr and/or his narrator are hardly the main characters in his novel. *Motti* revolves, as its titles suggests, around the eponymous protagonist. Schurr's Motti is quite nearly a loner. He has a dog, a single friend, and an infatuation with his neighbor, Ariella. Beyond this we know virtually nothing about his external reality. No mention of family, no mention of his relationship to the city or country in which he lives. From a slightly different and uncharitably critical perspective, we could even say that Motti is an incomplete character.

But Motti comes to life for the reader through our access to his inner world, where we find him endlessly preoccupied with his possible futures. In particular, Motti thinks about his future life with Ariella, about the passion they'll share, the difficulties they'll encounter, the family they'll make, and the inescapable end patiently waiting for both of them. Much of the events in *Motti* never happen at all, not even within the novel's imaginary world. Instead, we learn about Motti's life by learning about all the lives he imagines himself living in the future. Motti is hardly a hero in any conventional sense, but the reader identifies with him nevertheless, since we all live so much of our lives in the private ether of our endless speculations.

By casting as his protagonist a master of anticipation, speculation, and fantasy, by allowing possible futures to dwarf the immediate present again and again, Schurr reveals what it means to be a novelist in the first place. Or, from a perhaps more telling perspective, allows us to see the extent to which all of us are novelists of a sort: preoccupied with crafting our plot, overwhelmed by the burden of choosing from among the endless possibilities, and hard-pressed to come up with anything even approaching a satisfying ending. By portraying his protagonist in this way, Schurr both motivates his own asides and vindicates the frankness informing this playfulness as well.

■

I detect a certain inescapable melancholy at the center of all this, a feeling somewhere between despair and sorrow stemming from a shared failure to experience our external worlds as richly as we experience all the private events in our minds that never quite happen. The external real, it seems, will always pale next to the internal unreal. The main consolation, at least in Schurr's case, seems to be expressing this last sentiment so poignantly. *Motti*'s ultimate achievement (and the reason I hoped to translate it) is its language, which is at once precise and daring, sober and inventive, self-deprecating and ambitious. In a book so small that covers so much novelistic territory that has apparently already been covered (and dismissed as not just covered, but as exhausted, too), the pitfalls are numerous. But by finding just the right word time after time, by establishing and maintaining a singular tone located somewhere between amazement and defeat, Schurr justifies his refusal to follow so many often-imposing novelistic rules.

None of this is to say, of course, that all Hebrew novels, let alone all novels, should be like *Motti*. We should continue to read Hebrew novels to get The Story, we should read Yehoshua, Grossman, and Castel-Bloom if we really want to understand what life is truly like over there. But we should make room for something else, too, something utterly different, something concerned with a rich inner world somehow prior to the great, messy world outside. That a person could maintain the sensitive faculties necessary for detecting and then transcribing the elusive and fragile language of this private territory, all while living in that overwhelming and difficult reality called Israel, is all the more reason to read *Motti* with a serious and generous eye.

TODD HASAK-LOWY, 2011

HEBREW LITERATURE SERIES

The Hebrew Literature Series at Dalkey Archive Press makes available major works of Hebrew-language literature in English translation. Featuring exceptional authors at the forefront of Hebrew letters, the series aims to introduce the rich intellectual and aesthetic diversity of contemporary Hebrew writing and culture to English-language readers.

This series is published in collaboration with the Institute for the Translation of Hebrew Literature, at www.ithl.org.il. Thanks are also due to the Office of Cultural Affairs at the Consulate General of Israel, NY, for their support.

ASAF SCHURR was born in Jerusalem in 1976 and has a BA in philosophy and theater from the Hebrew University of Jerusalem. At present he is a translator and writes literary reviews for the Hebrew press. Schurr has received the Bernstein Prize (2007), the Minister of Culture Prize (2007) for *Amram*, and the Prime Minister's Prize for *Motti* (2008).

TODD HASAK-LOWY is Associate Professor of Hebrew Literature at the University of Florida. His first collection of short stories, *The Task of This Translator*, was published in 2005; his debut novel, *Captives*, appeared in 2008.

PETROS ABATZOGLOU, *What Does Mrs. Freeman Want?*
MICHAL AJVAZ, *The Golden Age.*
The Other City.
PIERRE ALBERT-BIROT, *Grabinoulor.*
YUZ ALESHKOVSKY, *Kangaroo.*
FELIPE ALFAU, *Chromos.*
Locos.
IVAN ÂNGELO, *The Celebration.*
The Tower of Glass.
DAVID ANTIN, *Talking.*
ANTÓNIO LOBO ANTUNES, *Knowledge of Hell.*
ALAIN ARIAS-MISSON, *Theatre of Incest.*
IFTIKHAR ARIF AND WAQAS KHWAJA, EDS., *Modern Poetry of Pakistan.*
JOHN ASHBERY AND JAMES SCHUYLER, *A Nest of Ninnies.*
GABRIELA AVIGUR-ROTEM, *Heatwave and Crazy Birds.*
HEIMRAD BÄCKER, *transcript.*
DJUNA BARNES, *Ladies Almanack.*
Ryder.
JOHN BARTH, *LETTERS.*
Sabbatical.
DONALD BARTHELME, *The King.*
Paradise.
SVETISLAV BASARA, *Chinese Letter.*
RENÉ BELLETTO, *Dying.*
MARK BINELLI, *Sacco and Vanzetti Must Die!*
ANDREI BITOV, *Pushkin House.*
ANDREJ BLATNIK, *You Do Understand.*
LOUIS PAUL BOON, *Chapel Road.*
My Little War.
Summer in Termuren.
ROGER BOYLAN, *Killoyle.*
IGNÁCIO DE LOYOLA BRANDÃO, *Anonymous Celebrity.*
The Good-Bye Angel.
Teeth under the Sun.
Zero.
BONNIE BREMSER, *Troia: Mexican Memoirs.*
CHRISTINE BROOKE-ROSE, *Amalgamemnon.*
BRIGID BROPHY, *In Transit.*
MEREDITH BROSNAN, *Mr. Dynamite.*
GERALD L. BRUNS, *Modern Poetry and the Idea of Language.*
EVGENY BUNIMOVICH AND J. KATES, EDS., *Contemporary Russian Poetry: An Anthology.*
GABRIELLE BURTON, *Heartbreak Hotel.*
MICHEL BUTOR, *Degrees.*
Mobile.
Portrait of the Artist as a Young Ape.
G. CABRERA INFANTE, *Infante's Inferno.*
Three Trapped Tigers.
JULIETA CAMPOS, *The Fear of Losing Eurydice.*
ANNE CARSON, *Eros the Bittersweet.*
ORLY CASTEL-BLOOM, *Dolly City.*
CAMILO JOSÉ CELA, *Christ versus Arizona.*
The Family of Pascual Duarte.
The Hive.
LOUIS-FERDINAND CÉLINE, *Castle to Castle.*
Conversations with Professor Y.
London Bridge.
Normance.
North.
Rigadoon.
HUGO CHARTERIS, *The Tide Is Right.*
JEROME CHARYN, *The Tar Baby.*
ERIC CHEVILLARD, *Demolishing Nisard.*
MARC CHOLODENKO, *Mordechai Schamz.*
JOSHUA COHEN, *Witz.*
EMILY HOLMES COLEMAN, *The Shutter of Snow.*
ROBERT COOVER, *A Night at the Movies.*
STANLEY CRAWFORD, *Log of the S.S. The Mrs Unguentine.*
Some Instructions to My Wife.
ROBERT CREELEY, *Collected Prose.*
RENÉ CREVEL, *Putting My Foot in It.*
RALPH CUSACK, *Cadenza.*
SUSAN DAITCH, *L.C.*
Storytown.
NICHOLAS DELBANCO, *The Count of Concord.*
Sherbrookes.
NIGEL DENNIS, *Cards of Identity.*
PETER DIMOCK, *A Short Rhetoric for Leaving the Family.*
ARIEL DORFMAN, *Konfidenz.*
COLEMAN DOWELL, *The Houses of Children.*
Island People.
Too Much Flesh and Jabez.
ARKADII DRAGOMOSHCHENKO, *Dust.*
RIKKI DUCORNET, *The Complete Butcher's Tales.*
The Fountains of Neptune.
The Jade Cabinet.
The One Marvelous Thing.
Phosphor in Dreamland.
The Stain.
The Word "Desire."
WILLIAM EASTLAKE, *The Bamboo Bed.*
Castle Keep.
Lyric of the Circle Heart.
JEAN ECHENOZ, *Chopin's Move.*
STANLEY ELKIN, *A Bad Man.*
Boswell: A Modern Comedy.
Criers and Kibitzers, Kibitzers and Criers.
The Dick Gibson Show.
The Franchiser.
George Mills.
The Living End.
The MacGuffin.
The Magic Kingdom.
Mrs. Ted Bliss.
The Rabbi of Lud.
Van Gogh's Room at Arles.
ANNIE ERNAUX, *Cleaned Out.*
LAUREN FAIRBANKS, *Muzzle Thyself.*
Sister Carrie.
LESLIE A. FIEDLER, *Love and Death in the American Novel.*
JUAN FILLOY, *Op Oloop.*
GUSTAVE FLAUBERT, *Bouvard and Pécuchet.*
KASS FLEISHER, *Talking out of School.*
FORD MADOX FORD, *The March of Literature.*
JON FOSSE, *Aliss at the Fire.*
Melancholy.
MAX FRISCH, *I'm Not Stiller.*
Man in the Holocene.

SELECTED DALKEY ARCHIVE PAPERBACKS

CARLOS FUENTES, *Christopher Unborn.*
  Distant Relations.
  Terra Nostra.
  Where the Air Is Clear.
JANICE GALLOWAY, *Foreign Parts.*
  The Trick Is to Keep Breathing.
WILLIAM H. GASS, *Cartesian Sonata*
  and Other Novellas.
  Finding a Form.
  A Temple of Texts.
  The Tunnel.
  Willie Masters' Lonesome Wife.
GÉRARD GAVARRY, *Hoppla! 1 2 3.*
  Making a Novel.
ETIENNE GILSON,
  The Arts of the Beautiful.
  Forms and Substances in the Arts.
C. S. GISCOMBE, *Giscome Road.*
  Here.
  Prairie Style.
DOUGLAS GLOVER, *Bad News of the Heart.*
  The Enamoured Knight.
WITOLD GOMBROWICZ,
  A Kind of Testament.
KAREN ELIZABETH GORDON,
  The Red Shoes.
GEORGI GOSPODINOV, *Natural Novel.*
JUAN GOYTISOLO, *Count Julian.*
  Exiled from Almost Everywhere.
  Juan the Landless.
  Makbara.
  Marks of Identity.
PATRICK GRAINVILLE, *The Cave of Heaven.*
HENRY GREEN, *Back.*
  Blindness.
  Concluding.
  Doting.
  Nothing.
JIŘÍ GRUŠA, *The Questionnaire.*
GABRIEL GUDDING,
  Rhode Island Notebook.
MELA HARTWIG, *Am I a Redundant*
  Human Being?
JOHN HAWKES, *The Passion Artist.*
  Whistlejacket.
ALEKSANDAR HEMON, ED.,
  Best European Fiction.
AIDAN HIGGINS, *A Bestiary.*
  Balcony of Europe.
  Bornholm Night-Ferry.
  Darkling Plain: Texts for the Air.
  Flotsam and Jetsam.
  Langrishe, Go Down.
  Scenes from a Receding Past.
  Windy Arbours.
KEIZO HINO, *Isle of Dreams.*
KAZUSHI HOSAKA, *Plainsong.*
ALDOUS HUXLEY, *Antic Hay.*
  Crome Yellow.
  Point Counter Point.
  Those Barren Leaves.
  Time Must Have a Stop.
NAOYUKI II, *The Shadow of a Blue Cat.*
MIKHAIL IOSSEL AND JEFF PARKER, EDS.,
  Amerika: Russian Writers View the
  United States.
GERT JONKE, *The Distant Sound.*
  Geometric Regional Novel.
  Homage to Czerny.
  The System of Vienna.

JACQUES JOUET, *Mountain R.*
  Savage.
  Upstaged.
CHARLES JULIET, *Conversations with*
  Samuel Beckett and Bram van
  Velde.
MIEKO KANAI, *The Word Book.*
YORAM KANIUK, *Life on Sandpaper.*
HUGH KENNER, *The Counterfeiters.*
  Flaubert, Joyce and Beckett:
  The Stoic Comedians.
  Joyce's Voices.
DANILO KIŠ, *Garden, Ashes.*
  A Tomb for Boris Davidovich.
ANITA KONKKA, *A Fool's Paradise.*
GEORGE KONRÁD, *The City Builder.*
TADEUSZ KONWICKI, *A Minor Apocalypse.*
  The Polish Complex.
MENIS KOUMANDAREAS, *Koula.*
ELAINE KRAF, *The Princess of 72nd Street.*
JIM KRUSOE, *Iceland.*
EWA KURYLUK, *Century 21.*
EMILIO LASCANO TEGUI, *On Elegance*
  While Sleeping.
ERIC LAURRENT, *Do Not Touch.*
HERVÉ LE TELLIER, *The Sextine Chapel.*
  A Thousand Pearls (for a Thousand
  Pennies)
VIOLETTE LEDUC, *La Bâtarde.*
EDOUARD LEVÉ, *Suicide.*
SUZANNE JILL LEVINE, *The Subversive*
  Scribe: Translating Latin
  American Fiction.
DEBORAH LEVY, *Billy and Girl.*
  Pillow Talk in Europe and Other
  Places.
JOSÉ LEZAMA LIMA, *Paradiso.*
ROSA LIKSOM, *Dark Paradise.*
OSMAN LINS, *Avalovara.*
  The Queen of the Prisons of Greece.
ALF MAC LOCHLAINN,
  The Corpus in the Library.
  Out of Focus.
RON LOEWINSOHN, *Magnetic Field(s).*
MINA LOY, *Stories and Essays of Mina Loy.*
BRIAN LYNCH, *The Winner of Sorrow.*
D. KEITH MANO, *Take Five.*
MICHELINE AHARONIAN MARCOM,
  The Mirror in the Well.
BEN MARCUS,
  The Age of Wire and String.
WALLACE MARKFIELD,
  Teitlebaum's Window.
  To an Early Grave.
DAVID MARKSON, *Reader's Block.*
  Springer's Progress.
  Wittgenstein's Mistress.
CAROLE MASO, *AVA.*
LADISLAV MATEJKA AND KRYSTYNA
  POMORSKA, EDS.,
  Readings in Russian Poetics:
  Formalist and Structuralist Views.
HARRY MATHEWS,
  The Case of the Persevering Maltese:
  Collected Essays.
  Cigarettes.
  The Conversions.
  The Human Country: New and
  Collected Stories.
  The Journalist.

FOR A FULL LIST OF PUBLICATIONS, VISIT:
www.dalkeyarchive.com

My Life in CIA.
Singular Pleasures.
The Sinking of the Odradek
  Stadium.
Tlooth.
20 Lines a Day.
JOSEPH MCELROY,
  Night Soul and Other Stories.
THOMAS MCGONIGLE,
  Going to Patchogue.
ROBERT L. MCLAUGHLIN, ED., *Innovations:*
  An Anthology of
  Modern & Contemporary Fiction.
ABDELWAHAB MEDDEB, *Talismano.*
HERMAN MELVILLE, *The Confidence-Man.*
AMANDA MICHALOPOULOU, *I'd Like.*
STEVEN MILLHAUSER,
  The Barnum Museum.
  In the Penny Arcade.
RALPH J. MILLS, JR.,
  Essays on Poetry.
MOMUS, *The Book of Jokes.*
CHRISTINE MONTALBETTI, *Western.*
OLIVE MOORE, *Spleen.*
NICHOLAS MOSLEY, *Accident.*
  Assassins.
  Catastrophe Practice.
  Children of Darkness and Light.
  Experience and Religion.
  God's Hazard.
  The Hesperides Tree.
  Hopeful Monsters.
  Imago Bird.
  Impossible Object.
  Inventing God.
  Judith.
  Look at the Dark.
  Natalie Natalia.
  Paradoxes of Peace.
  Serpent.
  Time at War.
  The Uses of Slime Mould:
  Essays of Four Decades.
WARREN MOTTE,
  Fables of the Novel: French Fiction
  since 1990.
  Fiction Now: The French Novel in
  the 21st Century.
  Oulipo: A Primer of Potential
  Literature.
YVES NAVARRE, *Our Share of Time.*
  Sweet Tooth.
DOROTHY NELSON, *In Night's City.*
  Tar and Feathers.
ESHKOL NEVO, *Homesick.*
WILFRIDO D. NOLLEDO, *But for the Lovers.*
FLANN O'BRIEN,
  At Swim-Two-Birds.
  At War.
  The Best of Myles.
  The Dalkey Archive.
  Further Cuttings.
  The Hard Life.
  The Poor Mouth.
  The Third Policeman.
CLAUDE OLLIER, *The Mise-en-Scène.*
  Wert and the Life Without End.
PATRIK OUŘEDNÍK, *Europeana.*
  The Opportune Moment, 1855.
BORIS PAHOR, *Necropolis.*

FERNANDO DEL PASO,
  News from the Empire.
  Palinuro of Mexico.
ROBERT PINGET, *The Inquisitory.*
  Mahu or The Material.
  Trio.
MANUEL PUIG,
  Betrayed by Rita Hayworth.
  The Buenos Aires Affair.
  Heartbreak Tango.
RAYMOND QUENEAU, *The Last Days.*
  Odile.
  Pierrot Mon Ami.
  Saint Glinglin.
ANN QUIN, *Berg.*
  Passages.
  Three.
  Tripticks.
ISHMAEL REED,
  The Free-Lance Pallbearers.
  The Last Days of Louisiana Red.
  Ishmael Reed: The Plays.
  Juice!
  Reckless Eyeballing.
  The Terrible Threes.
  The Terrible Twos.
  Yellow Back Radio Broke-Down.
JOÃO UBALDO RIBEIRO, *House of the*
  Fortunate Buddhas.
JEAN RICARDOU, *Place Names.*
RAINER MARIA RILKE, *The Notebooks of*
  Malte Laurids Brigge.
JULIÁN RÍOS, *The House of Ulysses.*
  Larva: A Midsummer Night's Babel.
  Poundemonium.
  Procession of Shadows.
AUGUSTO ROA BASTOS, *I the Supreme.*
DANIËL ROBBERECHTS,
  Arriving in Avignon.
JEAN ROLIN, *The Explosion of the*
  Radiator Hose.
OLIVIER ROLIN, *Hotel Crystal.*
ALIX CLEO ROUBAUD, *Alix's Journal.*
JACQUES ROUBAUD, *The Form of a*
  City Changes Faster, Alas, Than
  the Human Heart.
  The Great Fire of London.
  Hortense in Exile.
  Hortense Is Abducted.
  The Loop.
  The Plurality of Worlds of Lewis.
  The Princess Hoppy.
  Some Thing Black.
LEON S. ROUDIEZ, *French Fiction Revisited.*
RAYMOND ROUSSEL, *Impressions of Africa.*
VEDRANA RUDAN, *Night.*
STIG SÆTERBAKKEN, *Siamese.*
LYDIE SALVAYRE, *The Company of Ghosts.*
  Everyday Life.
  The Lecture.
  Portrait of the Writer as a
  Domesticated Animal.
  The Power of Flies.
LUIS RAFAEL SÁNCHEZ,
  Macho Camacho's Beat.
SEVERO SARDUY, *Cobra & Maitreya.*
NATHALIE SARRAUTE,
  Do You Hear Them?
  Martereau.
  The Planetarium.

SELECTED DALKEY ARCHIVE PAPERBACKS

ARNO SCHMIDT, *Collected Novellas.*
   Collected Stories.
   Nobodaddy's Children.
   Two Novels.
ASAF SCHURR, *Motti.*
CHRISTINE SCHUTT, *Nightwork.*
GAIL SCOTT, *My Paris.*
DAMION SEARLS, *What We Were Doing*
   and Where We Were Going.
JUNE AKERS SEESE,
   Is This What Other Women Feel Too?
   What Waiting Really Means.
BERNARD SHARE, *Inish.*
   Transit.
AURELIE SHEEHAN,
   Jack Kerouac Is Pregnant.
VIKTOR SHKLOVSKY, *Bowstring.*
   Knight's Move.
   A Sentimental Journey:
     Memoirs 1917–1922.
   Energy of Delusion: A Book on Plot.
   Literature and Cinematography.
   Theory of Prose.
   Third Factory.
   Zoo, or Letters Not about Love.
CLAUDE SIMON, *The Invitation.*
PIERRE SINIAC, *The Collaborators.*
JOSEF ŠKVORECKÝ, *The Engineer of*
   Human Souls.
GILBERT SORRENTINO,
   Aberration of Starlight.
   Blue Pastoral.
   Crystal Vision.
   Imaginative Qualities of Actual
     Things.
   Mulligan Stew.
   Pack of Lies.
   Red the Fiend.
   The Sky Changes.
   Something Said.
   Splendide-Hôtel.
   Steelwork.
   Under the Shadow.
W. M. SPACKMAN,
   The Complete Fiction.
ANDRZEJ STASIUK, *Fado.*
GERTRUDE STEIN,
   Lucy Church Amiably.
   The Making of Americans.
   A Novel of Thank You.
LARS SVENDSEN, *A Philosophy of Evil.*
PIOTR SZEWC, *Annihilation.*
GONÇALO M. TAVARES, *Jerusalem.*
   Learning to Pray in the Age of
     Technology.
LUCIAN DAN TEODOROVICI,
   Our Circus Presents . . .
STEFAN THEMERSON, *Hobson's Island.*
   The Mystery of the Sardine.
   Tom Harris.
JOHN TOOMEY, *Sleepwalker.*
JEAN-PHILIPPE TOUSSAINT,
   The Bathroom.
   Camera.
   Monsieur.
   Running Away.
   Self-Portrait Abroad.
   Television.
DUMITRU TSEPENEAG,
   Hotel Europa.

   The Necessary Marriage.
   Pigeon Post.
   Vain Art of the Fugue.
ESTHER TUSQUETS, *Stranded.*
DUBRAVKA UGRESIC,
   Lend Me Your Character.
   Thank You for Not Reading.
MATI UNT, *Brecht at Night.*
   Diary of a Blood Donor.
   Things in the Night.
ÁLVARO URIBE AND OLIVIA SEARS, EDS.,
   Best of Contemporary Mexican
     Fiction.
ELOY URROZ, *Friction.*
   The Obstacles.
LUISA VALENZUELA, *Dark Desires and*
   the Others.
   He Who Searches.
MARJA-LIISA VARTIO,
   The Parson's Widow.
PAUL VERHAEGHEN, *Omega Minor.*
BORIS VIAN, *Heartsnatcher.*
LLORENÇ VILLALONGA, *The Dolls' Room.*
ORNELA VORPSI, *The Country Where No*
   One Ever Dies.
AUSTRYN WAINHOUSE, *Hedyphagetica.*
PAUL WEST,
   Words for a Deaf Daughter & Gala.
CURTIS WHITE,
   America's Magic Mountain.
   The Idea of Home.
   Memories of My Father Watching TV.
   Monstrous Possibility: An Invitation
     to Literary Politics.
   Requiem.
DIANE WILLIAMS, *Excitability:*
   Selected Stories.
   Romancer Erector.
DOUGLAS WOOLF, *Wall to Wall.*
   Ya! & John-Juan.
JAY WRIGHT, *Polynomials and Pollen.*
   The Presentable Art of Reading
     Absence.
PHILIP WYLIE, *Generation of Vipers.*
MARGUERITE YOUNG, *Angel in the Forest.*
   Miss MacIntosh, My Darling.
REYOUNG, *Unbabbling.*
VLADO ŽABOT, *The Succubus.*
ZORAN ŽIVKOVIĆ, *Hidden Camera.*
LOUIS ZUKOFSKY, *Collected Fiction.*
SCOTT ZWIREN, *God Head.*